SO-AEA-532

Inside: Readers share their love stories.

Fun and romance in the snow . . .

I looked at her with alarm. "What are you doing?"

"What does it look like I'm doing?" Caitlin replied, arching her eyebrows. She bunched together a wad of snow and began squeezing it into a ball.

"Caitlin Dawes, you put that snowball down this instant, or I'll—"

"What?"

"Or I'll think of something."

"That's lame," Caitlin said with a laugh. She hurled the snowball at me. It socked me with a *thwack* right in the center of my chest.

I leaped to my feet. "That's it!" I shouted. "I warned you!" I dove toward her, tackling her to the ground.

We rolled around for a few moments, neither of us getting the upper hand. But finally I managed to flop on top of her.

As I gazed down at her flushed face I realized that she'd never looked more beautiful, more alive, than she did at that moment. So quickly—in just over a month—she had become my entire world.

A second later I was completely lost in the all-encompassing passion of kissing her soft mouth.

Which tasted clean and cold, like freshly fallen snow.

Love Stories

A Song for Caitlin

J. E. Bright

BANTAM BOOKS
NEW YORK · TORONTO · LONDON · SYDNEY · AUCKLAND

Thanks to Jason, for helping me with the music; to Geri Lynn, for cluing me in to Boulder hot spots; and to David, for describing a Bach cello suite. Any mistakes are mine, not theirs. Big thanks also go to B. J.; Mom and Dad, for temporary subsidy; to Raina, for being a patient, creative editor; to David, again, for dealing with my freak-outs; and to Joshua, for inspiration.

RL 6, age 12 and up

A SONG FOR CAITLIN

A Bantam Book / August 1998

*Produced by 17th Street Productions,
a division of Daniel Weiss Associates, Inc.
33 West 17th Street
New York, NY 10011.
Cover photography by Michael Segal.*

ISBN: 0-553-49248-9

Published simultaneously in the United States and Canada

PRINTED IN THE UNITED STATES OF AMERICA

OPM   0 9 8 7 6 5 4 3 2 1

Prologue

H OW CAN I go on when my girlfriend is
dead?

I can't. It's impossible. I don't even feel like
myself anymore. I mean, when I see myself in
the mirror, I still *look* the same—blue eyes and
dark hair and all that, but I *feel* as though a
large part of me died along with Caitlin. I
loved her more than I ever thought I could
love anyone. She passed away just over a
month ago, and every day since has been almost unbearable.

Right now I'm in the backstage tent at a
rave in the mountains near Boulder, Colorado,
about forty minutes away from where I live.
I'm unpacking my keyboard, attaching it to its
stand, getting it ready to carry out onstage in a
few hours. My band—Tomorrowland—plays

electronica music. Future sounds. At one point in my life I looked forward to the future. But now I can't give up the past. Because that means letting go of Caitlin.

I think about her all the time. Even with my best friends—the other members of my band—setting up our gear around me, I'm swamped with memories. A few hours ago I thought I could go through with this, getting up onstage and making that crowd move, think, and feel with our music. But now I'm not sure I can. I'm frozen with the amp plugs in my hand.

"Brad? You okay, man?" Jeff Pilotte, my best friend and Tomorrowland's drummer, asks me.

"I'm fine," I tell Jeff.

"You hear these lame-os?" he asks, gesturing toward the stage behind the tent wall. "They call this music?"

I nod. "They *are* pretty bad."

Jeff grins. "We'll blow them away," he says. "They can't touch our originality."

"Uh-huh," I reply.

He studies me for a moment. "You sure you're okay?"

"I *said* I was fine," I answer, a little more sharply than I intended.

"Okay, cool." Jeff leaves me to my keyboard and goes to check out his drum kit over by the rack of pipes and other gizmos he uses

2

for alternative percussion. Jeff's the one who convinced me to perform tonight. He said that the band needed me, that I couldn't avoid my life, and that Caitlin would want me to go on playing music.

Jeff is right. The band does need me—I'm their lead singer, after all. And I can't avoid my life, as much as I sometimes want to. Caitlin *wouldn't* want me to stop living for anything, even her. I know all that.

But none of those reasons matter, not now. Because I lied. I'm *not* fine.

I stare down at the amp plugs. Figuring out where they go seems like too much of an effort, so I drop them on the scrubby grass floor of the tent. I can't go on tonight. I just can't. It's too soon.

I look around the tent. I have to tell my friends I can't perform. But the faces of all four guys—Jeff, Ryan Benton, Andre Fink, and Kenny Waters—are happy and excited. They're totally psyched to play. I hate to let them down—the rush of performing onstage is indescribably cool. I press a few keys on my synth, hoping to feel the buzz that will open into that rush of energy once I'm in front of the audience. But I feel nothing.

I step toward the guys. I'll apologize, say Caitlin's name. They'll be disappointed, but they'll understand. They have to.

Before I can open my mouth, Ryan, our deejay, presses a button to check his sound levels. Softly, over the bad music of the current band, a sample of Caitlin's cello fills the tent.

I stop moving, my heart pounding. Caitlin was a better musician than I can ever hope to be. Her cello playing was so incredible that even now, as the sample fills my ears, I can barely catch my breath. Caitlin put everything she felt into her music. She played with her whole self, all her emotions, all her humor, all her sadness, and all her troubles. My legs feel weak.

Quickly I stumble over to a metal folding chair and collapse onto it. I close my eyes and drink in her sounds. Each note reminds me of something about Caitlin—her wicked, teasing grin, her rich brown eyes, the childlike way she held a cup two-handed when she drank, the salty-sweet taste of her lips. Thoughts of Caitlin flood me as I listen, months of memories—the best time of my life.

Sinking on the strains of her cello, I fall back into the past, back to the beginning when we first met, wishing I could stay there forever. . . .

One

WE'RE DYING UP *here*, I thought.

It was a Saturday night, and I stood onstage at a little café-club in Boulder called Penny Lane. The place was usually filled with hippies, but one night a week they had dance bands. We'd been lucky enough to win this slot on their audition night. If we were good, we'd get to play again—on dance night.

Outside, the October night was clear and crisp—and the crowd inside was just as chilly. They were definitely underwhelmed with our performance. During the first two songs most of the people barely paid attention, and those who were looking up at us weren't dancing at all. The majority of the upturned faces seemed downright bored.

Not that I blamed them. I wasn't impressed

with us either. All the funky tribal drumbeats and samples that had seemed so cool when we'd practiced them in my garage suddenly sounded really flat.

Now, in the third song, Jeff was supposed to change his tempo from a heartbeat rhythm—120 beats per minute—and bring it up to a much whirlier speed—136 bpm. For some reason he couldn't seem to get his drumming up to the necessary peak. He was probably just nervous. But the crescendos were lame, and that threw off the rest of the band.

I winced as Andre totally flubbed a progression on his bass. That was completely unlike him—he was usually an excellent player. I glanced over at him, and he met my gaze with his intense black eyes, raising his thick dark eyebrows and shrugging. *Sorry, dude,* he seemed to be saying. *But right now we're all up the creek without a paddle.*

Great. So both our drummer and bassist were shaky. Without a tight rhythm section we were in deep trouble.

At least Kenny was doing fine on keyboard. I played the top melody on my synth while he backed me up with whooshy ambient sounds on his. He played ten different instruments besides his synth, weird little instruments that added a cool spark of originality to Tomorrowland's sound. I watched out of the corner of my eye as he pulled a tin whistle out of his shirt pocket and played a high little trill on it, weaving it neatly under my keyboard line.

I nodded with satisfaction. *That* was getting some attention. We were starting to sound good. Jeff and Andre pulled themselves back into the groove. Tomorrowland was on track again.

Then disaster struck.

This cute girl with long chestnut hair and a killer smile pushed up to the front of the stage. Kenny's eyes zeroed in on her immediately, and I nearly groaned out loud.

Kenny was a total dog. Most of the time he was off in his own world, but when a pretty girl was involved, he lost control.

I exchanged a glance with Ryan, the computer expert who managed all our samples and programmed our trickier sounds. Ryan was pretty much a geeky genius, with dirty thick glasses and no sense of style. But he was a good guy, and his girlfriend, Beth, was pretty cool. He and I had discussed our worries over Kenny's love life before. Not that I really cared about his girl problems—unless it affected the band. Which I knew would happen right now.

Sure enough, Kenny went into overdrive

trying to impress the girl. He blasted into his whistle . . . and all that came out was a nasty, shrill squeak.

The music faltered. I felt the crowd close up against us. Some guy even laughed.

I shook my head in disgust. The whole instrumental opening was supposed to bring the crowd up to a trancelike state, ready to hear our message in the lyrics. But forget that. We'd be lucky if they didn't start throwing stuff.

And now I had to *sing?*

Be professional, I reminded myself. *Just get through this.*

The song—which I'd written the lyrics for—was called "The Enforcers." It was a warning against allowing the government to take control of your life. So in a deep, menacing growl I chanted:

> The police enforce the laws—
> find a fool to take a fall,
> slam cuffs around the hands
> of anyone who takes a stand. . . .

The music swelled behind me. Ryan blasted out a sample of a siren that he'd electronically altered—slowing it down to make it even more ominous. And Jeff's drumming began to sound like a march, to give off the

8

sense that armies of police were advancing. I sang:

> Don't let them tell you what to do
> 'cause soon enough they'll come after you.

What's going on? I thought, worried. The song was moving along just like we'd planned, but for some reason it sounded lame.

What do I really have against the police? I thought as I listened to Kenny peep away on his whistle. The only time I'd ever dealt with the cops was when I was nine and they brought back my stolen bike. The Boulder police had always been perfectly nice to me.

I took a deep breath and glared out at the audience in what I hoped was a direct, intense stare as I got ready to chant the central chorus:

> The Enforcers make the rules.
> Rules are made to be broken.
> Break them.
> Break them.

These lyrics are stupid, I realized suddenly. I mean, I didn't believe that *all* rules should be broken. It had just sounded cool when I wrote the words.

Nobody was dancing, even though the beat was funky and fast. I chanted the chorus again, trying to sound dangerous and meaningful. But except for a few girls swaying a little in the back of the club, everyone stared up at me with bored faces. The club manager actually yawned.

"Break them, break them," I sang. But my voice sounded worried instead of menacing, dumb instead of profound. I couldn't wait for the song to be over—so I could get offstage.

Finally we wound down to a finish. Over the last notes Ryan played a sample of the screams of a riot—sirens and police megaphones—all distorted. Then he cut it off with a snap, and we all stopped playing our instruments. In my garage that abrupt ending had sounded cool, but now it just seemed dorky.

For a moment there was complete silence. Then the crowd applauded indifferently for a few seconds.

"Thank you," I called into the mike. "Good night! We're Tomorrowland!" Penny Lane's deejay immediately put on a CD.

I started to dismantle my keyboard, knowing there was no hope that we'd impressed the booker enough for him to sign us up for another gig. Tomorrowland's audition for dance band night was a big bust.

"Did you see that girl?" Kenny asked. He came up behind me and stared over my shoulder into the crowd. I could smell the faint whiff

10

of incense that always lingered around him. "Man, she's incredible. And she's totally into me, I could tell. She wants me."

I bit back a nasty reply. If he'd been concentrating on the music instead of watching some girl, we wouldn't have lost the rhythm. "Whatever," I said.

Kenny gave me a shove. "Don't pretend you didn't see her, Brad," he said. "She was *primo*. I saw you checking her out. But she only had eyes for me."

"I saw her," I growled, "but unlike you, I was actually trying to play a *song* up there." I lifted my keyboard from its stand and stalked offstage.

Kenny followed me. "Just admit it, Brad. Admit she's a babe, and I'll leave you alone."

I stopped beside my keyboard case in the wings. "You're entitled to your opinions," I replied.

Kenny laughed. "That's what I love about you, Brad-dude," he said. "You're always so open and honest with yourself."

"What's that supposed to mean?" I demanded.

Instead of answering, Kenny let out a little yelp. "There she is," he breathed.

I glanced over to where he was staring and saw the girl he was talking about. She *was* cute. She was wearing a little red sweater with these fat black stripes and dark velvety pants. Her chestnut hair was long and full. The girl smiled as she noticed us checking her out, her whole face lighting up.

Shaking my head, I turned back to my keyboard case. Sure, she was pretty, but she probably had the brain of a flea. A dead flea. Anyone who could smile that effortlessly obviously wasn't facing reality with any intelligence.

"That's all the invitation I need," Kenny whispered. "Wish me luck."

"Luck," I told him. He pushed past me and headed straight for her.

I knelt down and secured my keyboard in its case, wrapping the cords up neatly and tucking them into their slots. *What am I even doing here?* I wondered. *Maybe my mother is right that this music thing is a waste of time. Maybe I should just forget about it since nobody thinks we're any good anyway.*

I took a deep breath as I closed the case. *Failure,* I thought, letting out a huge sigh. Tomorrowland wasn't going anywhere—except Yesterdayville. Better just face the facts and get on with our lives. I turned around to go collect my keyboard stand from the stage.

"What was that for?" a female voice asked from behind me.

"What?" I turned.

It was the girl Kenny was after. She looked even prettier up close.

"That big sigh," she said, smiling warmly. "What did it mean?"

"Nothing," I replied. I glanced over to the other side of the club and saw Kenny glaring at me. "It was just a sigh," I told her.

The girl's rich dark eyes searched my face. "Seems to me that it meant, 'Oh, well, guess it's over,'" she observed. "Like you're giving up."

"Um, yeah," I said. "Yeah, I guess that's pretty much it."

She shook her head. "You shouldn't. Give up, I mean. Do you mind . . ." Her voice trailed off.

"What?"

"Can I tell you what I thought? About your performance tonight?"

"Sure, whatever," I said.

She studied me for a moment. "What I really thought, or would you just like praise?" she asked. "I can do either."

"What you really thought," I answered quickly. "I don't need anyone kissing up to me. And it doesn't matter anyway. I'm giving up, remember?"

"No, you're not. You're too good to give up. Your problem is that you're not letting yourself *feel* the music," she said, watching me carefully.

"Huh?" *Feel the music?* What was this girl talking about? "I mean, what makes you say that?"

She blushed. "It seemed tense, too thought out," she explained. "I could read it in your body language. It's not just that you're not feeling it. You . . ." She lowered her eyes to the floor, apparently trying to find the right words. "You don't *believe* it."

I blinked. She was right. Or I thought she was—if I was understanding her correctly. I mean, in some ways this girl seemed to be speaking in another language or something. Trying to cover my confusion, I said, "I guess that's pretty right on. Although it's kinda harsh."

"Sorry." She blushed again, more deeply this time. "I can be too direct sometimes. I didn't mean to offend you." She gave me a small smile. "But why do you care, if you're quitting anyway?"

"Well," I replied, "I might not quit. You never know."

The girl laughed. "You're *not* going to quit," she insisted. "That would be stupid. You've just got to open yourself up while you're playing."

And how in the world do I do that? I thought. But I couldn't seem to make myself talk over the lump in my throat. I'd never reacted this way to a girl before.

She was about to say something else, but another girl appeared behind her—a girl with the same chestnut hair and big eyes. Her sister,

I guessed. "Caitlin, we'll miss our ride," she said abruptly. "We don't want to get stranded here."

Her name was Caitlin. I made a point of remembering that. *Caitlin.*

"Okay," Caitlin replied. Then she turned back to me. "I've got to go," she said, a note of regret in her voice.

"That's cool," I said. My words sounded funny to me—my throat was suddenly dry.

Caitlin waved as she began to follow her sister. "See you around," she called back.

"Yeah!" I shouted in reply.

I stared after Caitlin until she vanished into the crowd. Then I stared at where she'd been standing earlier. I don't know how much time passed before I noticed Jeff standing right beside me, grinning.

"Hey, man, I have a message from Kenny," he reported.

"Oh, yeah?" It took me a second, but I managed to focus in on Jeff's face.

"Yeah," he replied with a chuckle. "He wants to know what you think you're doing, trying to steal his girl."

"Please," I said, rolling my eyes.

"I know, the guy's out of his mind," Jeff agreed. "Like he had some claim on her. So what did you two talk about anyway?"

"Nothing much," I answered, rubbing the

base of my palm over my forehead. "We talked about the band, mostly."

"She say anything interesting?"

"I don't know," I told him. I paused for a moment, wondering if I should mention Caitlin's suggestions. "No, not really," I said. "Nothing important."

"Oh."

I sighed. The truth was, Caitlin's confusing words were stuck in my brain. "Jeff? Let me ask you something."

"Shoot."

"Do you think . . ." I ran my hand through my thick brown hair. "Do you think I'm not *feeling* the music when I sing?" Jeff raised his eyebrows in surprise, and I immediately felt stupid for asking. "Oh, never mind."

Jeff laughed. "What did that girl say to you?"

"Nothing," I answered defensively. "Nothing, really."

"Feeling the music, huh?" Jeff scratched his head. "Brad-man, you getting all gushy on us? Where's the guy who's always telling me emotions get in the way? Where's the guy who always says—"

"Forget it," I interrupted. "I've got to get my rack."

"Brad," Jeff called after me, but I pushed past him toward the stage.

What does Caitlin know anyway? I thought as I dismantled my keyboard stand. She'd never even met me before!

But as I worked, my mind drifted. She might be a complete stranger, but I couldn't get the image of Caitlin's warm smile and intelligent brown eyes out of my mind.

I shook my head. Beautiful or not, I wasn't going to think about her anymore. My last girlfriend, Sandy, who I dated for about two months, had this annoying habit of constantly *picking* at me, of always asking me too many questions. I'd ended it about five months ago when I just stopped calling her.

I could tell that this girl would do the same thing, trying to figure me out. Sure, Caitlin was gorgeous, but I didn't need anyone poking their nose into my business.

I carried the metal tubes of the keyboard rack down to their case.

No, I really didn't need that kind of attention at all.

Especially not from someone as obviously insightful as Caitlin.

Two

ON MONDAY AFTER school I was practicing the keyboard in my bedroom. My mother insisted that I connect headphones to it whenever I played in the house so as not to disturb her. I had them on even though she wouldn't be home from work for another twenty minutes—it had just gotten to be a habit.

I was playing a short repetition of melody, hoping for inspiration. I wanted to fix all the problems I'd noticed at Penny Lane, but I couldn't figure out how to start.

After a few minutes of concentrating I glanced around my room. I'd moved down to the basement two years ago, right after the divorce. My old room was right next to my parents' room, and sleeping there reminded me of all the times I'd lain awake listening to their fights.

Anyway, this bedroom was big, almost the size of our living room. The only other things in the basement were the garage and the laundry room. It was kind of like a sanctuary for me.

In one corner was a big double bed (unmade, of course) beside a dresser and a desk littered with papers and schoolbooks. The whole length of one wall was taken up by a couch Jeff and I had dragged in there. Across from that was a tiny, ancient TV that still worked well enough if you didn't mind watching cable with random green and red splotches.

My keyboard and musical equipment were lined up against the fourth wall, underneath three hanging racks of CDs. I had a *lot* of CDs—a couple hundred.

I shook my head. I wasn't getting any work done on my music. I was just staring around my room, trying to avoid thinking about her.

Caitlin.

I kept replaying the sudden glow of her smile, the rich brown of her eyes. . . .

Which was stupid. I didn't even know if she liked me. And all she had really done was criticize my band. I probably would never see her again anyway. . . .

I played the melodic line again. *I can be*

real, I told myself. *I can live my lyrics; I can believe in them. I'll show her.*

But no words sprang to mind. What subject should I sing about? I stopped playing and stared down at my fingers.

Suddenly I felt hands pull off my headphones from behind. I turned around in surprise—and came face-to-face with my mother.

"Mom!" I complained, taking the headphones out of her hands. "You scared me."

She was wearing her work clothes—a very professional-looking brown suit. Her dark hair was neatly sculpted as always, but she looked tired. She had black circles under her eyes. But those had been there ever since the divorce, ever since she'd thrown all her energy into her job. Now she worked too hard and didn't get enough sleep. At least her career wasn't suffering—she was up for a partnership in her law firm next year.

"Brad, don't you have homework?" she asked.

I groaned. "Nothing major," I replied. "I can do it quick after dinner. No problem."

She crossed her arms over her chest. "Homework shouldn't be *no problem,*" she said. "Not if you take your future seriously. Aren't your classes challenging enough?"

Not this speech again. I turned back to my

keyboard. "They're fine," I replied. "I'm doing fine. Don't worry about it."

"Of course I worry about it," my mother said. "It's time to start thinking about getting into a good college. I'd like to see you motivated about your future. If you would just stop wasting your time with this silly music—"

"Mom, please," I snapped.

We stood there in silence. Most of the time we got along fine, just sort of leaving each other alone. I hated it when she got into this worrying-about-my-future mode.

I heard her let out a big sigh. "So school was good, then," she said.

"Fine," I told her without turning around. "It was fine." I rolled my eyes. That's all my mother and I ever talked about—my day at school or her day at work. Ever since my father moved out, my mother, always stoic and reserved, had sort of cut herself off from other people. Including me.

But I couldn't really blame her. The divorce had been a horrible time for all of us. My father had moved to New York. I hardly ever spoke to him. He didn't seem to want to be a part of my life anymore. Of course that sucked, but there was nothing I could do about it. It was his problem, not mine.

I turned to face my mother. "Don't worry

about my homework, Mom," I said. "I've got it under control."

"All right." She gave me a slight nod. "Dinner will be ready in about an hour," she added.

"Sounds good."

"Okay," she said. Then she walked out of my bedroom.

Dealing with my mother kind of brought me down, but I pushed it all out of my head. I didn't want to think about my mother, or my father, or what had happened between them. Why should I?

Shaking my head to clear the miserable thoughts, I tried to concentrate on writing new, lived-in, honest lyrics.

But my mind was a total blank.

"Okay," Jeff said on Thursday afternoon, leaning forward on the small coffee-stained table at Café Roma. "We all agree that the music's not working yet. So what do we do about it?"

"We need to get more *real*," I told everybody. The guys all turned to face me, surprised expressions on their faces.

"What do you mean?" Kenny asked.

I tilted my small wooden chair back on two legs. "I think we need to be more honest. I don't mean we should be *embarrassing*, but . . ." My voice trailed away.

Ryan took off his glasses and wiped them on his shirt. "But we do need to write music from the heart," he finished for me. "Personal and meaningful, but still cool . . . right?"

I let my chair drop back down with a thud. "I guess. 'From the heart' sounds cheesy, but I suppose that's the basic idea."

"Makes sense," Jeff said, nodding.

"The question is, what should the songs be about?" I asked.

Everyone fell silent.

Then Kenny piped up. "Pets!" he exclaimed. He drained the last of his *caffè latte*—even though he was already jittering in his chair. "That's totally it! Everybody has pets. And people, like, really *care* about their dogs and cats."

I shook my head. Writing a song about pets was an incredibly stupid idea.

"Uh . . . Porno for Pyros already has a song called 'Pets,'" Jeff reminded him.

"That's right," I put in quickly. "Any other ideas?"

As Kenny pouted, the rest of the guys grew quiet again. I traced an old coffee stain ring on the wooden table with my finger.

Andre shifted in his seat. I glanced at him— the guy barely ever spoke, but he actually looked as though he might say something.

"Love," Andre murmured.

Jeff groaned. "Anything but that," he said, rolling his eyes. "Love's *so* overdone. I'm sick of bands whining about love this and love that and my girlfriend left me. It's so *tired*."

Jeff had never had a girlfriend. Outside of his friends—which was pretty much the four of us—he was painfully shy and awkward.

"I think it's a great idea," Kenny put in. "Babes totally dig love songs. Imagine how lucky I'd get if I told a girl that a song was about her?"

Typical Kenny. He had a point, though. Love songs were practically the foundation of music. But writing about love seemed so . . . revealing.

"I'm not sure," I began. "It *is* overdone—"

"It's a great idea," Ryan broke in. "I know Beth would love it if I put her in a song—like maybe even use a sample of her voice. Plus electronica bands usually stay away from love songs, so we'd be doing something kind of new."

"Cool," Andre said.

Two words from Andre in the same hour! Love must really mean something to him. I shouldn't have been surprised—girls fell for Andre's dark, mysterious thing all the time.

"Come on, Brad," Kenny added. "*You* don't believe in love, but the rest of us do."

"Love?" I teased. "Is that what you call your constant search for *sex?*"

25

"Harsh," Kenny replied, smiling.

"So love it is," Ryan declared.

"Whoo-hoo!" Kenny cried. "I'm going to be *drowning* in babes!"

Jeff sighed. "Fine," he muttered. "Whatever."

I shoved his shoulder. "Hey," I said. "It's not like it affects the drumming, dude. We still need a funky beat."

"I guess," he said.

This will be cool, I decided. Writing about love wasn't *such* an awful idea—I could write lyrics about *not* being able to fall in love. Or not believing in love . . .

My gaze wandered as I thought. My eyes fell on a small table near the door of the café. Was that who I thought it was?

Yes.

Caitlin. She was sitting alone, reading a book.

I watched as she turned a page—even though the café was kind of noisy, she seemed to be deep in concentration. She was stunning. Still reading, she reached for her cup of cappuccino and took a sip. My heart stopped beating for a moment when she licked a spot of foam off the rim of the cup.

"Yo, Brad!" Kenny called across the table. "You just see a ghost?"

I ignored him and stood up, scraping the legs of my chair against the tile floor.

Ryan craned his skinny neck around. "It's that girl," he said. "From our gig. The pretty one who Kenny struck out with."

Jeff laughed, and Kenny scowled down at the table.

"Sorry, man," Ryan apologized to Kenny. "But she was a lot more interested in talking to Brad."

"Uh, um . . . ," I mumbled. "Catch you guys later."

And then I found myself walking toward Caitlin's table. She looked great, dressed in a soft, dark brown sweater, with this big silver ball dangling from the end of a black cord around her neck. Her hair was casually pushed back with a dark red headband. "Good to see you again," I said, stopping in front of her.

Caitlin glanced up, startled. Something inside the silver ball tinkled musically as she moved. "Oh . . . hi!" she said. A big smile crept across her face.

"You remember me, right?"

Caitlin closed her book, keeping her finger inside it as a bookmark. "Of course. But I, um . . ." She blushed. "I'm really sorry, but I think I've forgotten your name."

I laughed. "I don't think I told you, so how could you forget? I'm Brad. Brad Myers."

"Hi, Brad," she said, smiling again. I got a

weird little thrill from hearing her say my name. She tilted her head at the empty chair across from her. "You want to sit down?"

I sat. "You're Caitlin, right?"

"Caitlin Dawes," she answered with a nod. "How'd you know?"

"I'm psychic," I replied. I didn't know where I got that reply, but it just came out.

Caitlin leaned forward. "Wow," she said, widening her eyes in fake amazement. "That's a great power to have. Must help out a lot on tests and stuff."

"It does. It's a very useful gift."

"I bet. So . . ." She adjusted her headband. "What am I thinking right now?"

I pretended to concentrate, rubbing my hand over my chin. "You're thinking . . . wait, it's coming to me. . . . You're thinking, 'How'd he *really* know my name? Because if he's psychic, then I'm Kathie Lee Gifford.'"

Caitlin giggled. "Maybe you are psychic," she said. "That was pretty close. Although I definitely wasn't thinking about Kathie Lee. So how *did* you know my name?"

"That girl said it," I replied. "At Penny Lane, the girl who you left with. I figured she was your sister, right?"

"Very good," Caitlin told me. "I'd say that proves you're psychic except that I know Becca and I look alike."

28

You're prettier, I wanted to say, but I had to keep *some* cool. "Yeah, you do," I said. "So . . . you don't go to Boulder High, do you? I haven't seen you around school."

"No," Caitlin replied. "We—I mean my family—just moved here in August."

"From where?"

"California. San Diego. I'm not sorry we left—San Diego was really uptight. I like Boulder so far. And the September School, where I go now, has a much better music program than my old school."

The September School was this alternative arts high school. It's almost impossible to get into. Caitlin must be really talented. "What do you play?" I asked.

"Cello," she answered, her eyes lighting up. "Classical mostly, but I love every kind of music. All music comes from the same place—for me anyway. Rock, jazz, blues, classical . . . even dance music. Maybe especially dance music. I have no time for music snobs."

I could believe that. It was hard to picture Caitlin being snobby about anything. "That's cool," I said. "Cello, wow. No wonder."

"No wonder what?" Caitlin asked.

"No wonder you knew what you were talking about the other day. You know, when you were telling me what's wrong with my band."

Caitlin ducked her head and blushed. She did that a lot, I'd noticed. "Sorry about that," she said. "I thought you guys were good. I didn't mean to be so harsh."

"Don't worry about it," I told her. "I'm still not exactly sure what you meant, though."

"You'll figure it out," she replied. "But I shouldn't have said anything. I should save my criticism for people who know me better." She ripped off a piece of napkin and stuck it into her book, slipping her finger out from between the pages. "I mean, that kind of thing should only come from . . . a friend."

We sat in silence for a moment as I tried to think of something to talk about.

"Uh . . . so where do you live?" I asked finally. "I mean, what street?"

"Not too far away," she said. "It's like a ten-minute drive; Southgate Road. It's a nice enough house—"

"Southgate!" I interrupted. "I live on Wesley, just around the corner from Southgate. And hey, I bet I know which house you moved into—the white one with the big shrubs, right? That one's been for sale for a while."

"Exactly," Caitlin said. "Wesley, huh? Which house?"

I shifted in my seat. "Twenty-eight. The yellow one in the middle of the block."

Caitlin smiled. "Oh, the yellow one. I wondered who was brave enough to paint their house such a bright color. I mean, I like it. It's just very bright."

I chuckled. "My father loves that color," I said. "He painted it yellow right before he moved out. My mother . . ." My voice trailed off. Had I really just told her my father moved out? I *never* discussed my parents' divorce. Not with anyone.

"When did your parents split up?" Caitlin asked.

"Two years ago."

"That must have been rough."

I clasped my hands together in my lap. "Yeah, it was. On my mom especially. She really threw herself into work—"

"It must have been rough on *you*," Caitlin cut in.

I met Caitlin's deep brown eyes. "Yeah," I replied quietly. "It was." I shook my head and took a deep breath. "Can we talk about something else?"

Caitlin shrugged. "Sure," she said. "What?"

"It's your turn to think up something." I felt a little angry with myself for getting all emotional. This girl was *dangerous*.

"Okay." She thought for a second, looking up toward the low ceiling of the café. "Okay. How about an invitation?"

"An invitation to what?"

"Well, I'm giving my first cello recital on Sunday. You could come if you want. It's in the September School music auditorium. Or you don't have to come if you don't want to."

I hesitated. Caitlin was the most beautiful girl I'd ever met in my life. I wanted to get to know her better. But she kept making me feel so strange—I'd already told her more about myself than I ever told anyone. Private stuff. Feelings that were no one's business.

"Really, you don't have to," Caitlin said as my hesitation lingered. "Forget I said anything. I shouldn't have asked—"

"No, no," I broke in. "I'll definitely be there. You can count on it." Where had *that* come from?

"Great!" Caitlin said with a big smile. "Sunday at four o'clock."

"All right," I said. We just sat there grinning stupidly at each other for a second.

"I should go," she said finally. "My parents want me home by six for dinner. But let's exchange phone numbers in case you can't make the recital for some reason, or get lost, or whatever."

"All right," I said, wishing she didn't have to leave.

Caitlin fished around in her jacket pocket and pulled out a black pen. "I knew I had this in there," she muttered. She grabbed a napkin that had only a little coffee on it and scribbled down her number. Then she held out the pen toward me. "Here—write yours."

I reached to take it. My fingers accidentally brushed hers.

A tingling bolt of pure electricity shot up my arm.

Three

"HELLO. MAY I speak to Brad, please?"

"Yeah?" I responded over the phone. "This is me."

"Oh, hi! It's Caitlin."

I turned away from my keyboard, happy to hear her voice. "Hey—how's it going?"

"Oh, busy," she replied. "The recital's in, what . . . two hours? So I've been practicing like a maniac."

The recital? In two hours! I'd totally forgotten it was today. My hand tightened around the receiver in a slight panic, but I tried to keep cool and act as if I'd completely remembered. "I never practice before a show," I said. "I just try to relax."

"Maybe you *should* practice," Caitlin teased. "Maybe it would've helped."

"Hey, watch it," I growled.

She laughed. "You know I'm just joking."

"I know."

Caitlin laughed again. "So," she said. "I was calling to see if you needed directions to my school. That is, if you're still coming."

Was I still going? I had to say something. "No," I replied, flustered. "I mean, yes." I groaned. "I mean, yes, I'm coming. No, I don't need directions. I know how to get there." I figured it was better to just tell her I'd be there and then worry about the details later.

"Great!" she exclaimed. "I'm so psyched you'll get to hear us play. The whole show will be excellent. I know for a fact that the other performers have all been working really hard."

"I don't care about the others," I said, surprising myself. "I'm going to hear you." That was the truth—*if* I went, it would be to see her.

"Really?"

I swallowed. What was I getting myself into? "Really," I replied.

"Great. Well, I need to go practice again, but I'll see you later."

"Sure."

"Cool," Caitlin responded. "Bye."

"Bye."

As I hung up the phone I cursed myself for forgetting about Caitlin's recital. And now I'd told her that I'd definitely be there when I wasn't quite sure if that was how I wanted to spend my afternoon. I mean, it would be cool to see Caitlin again, but I wasn't really in the mood to sit through a long classical concert, bored out of my mind.

I headed upstairs to the kitchen. As I fixed myself a sandwich I decided that after getting some food in my stomach and taking a short nap, I'd feel energized and ready to go to Caitlin's recital.

It was a good theory. Except my nap didn't turn out to be short. When I woke up on the couch in a haze, the living room clock read 3:47.

I sat up straight, now fully awake. What should I do? The concert was in fifteen minutes—there was still time to make it if I hurried. I'd told her I'd be there.

But then again—getting up from the couch, putting on my shoes, driving over to the September School—it was the last thing I felt like doing. Besides, as attracted to Caitlin as I was, I still barely knew her. She was just a girl. This was nothing to get all worked up about.

Caitlin would understand. How could she expect anyone to sit through a recital in the middle of the afternoon? That was a lot to ask. She probably wouldn't even notice I wasn't there. She probably wouldn't even care.

I settled into the couch and turned on the TV with the remote. I channel-surfed for a couple of minutes, not really focusing on any of the shows I passed through. *Maybe I should go,* I thought, switching to MTV, *maybe it wouldn't be so bad.* I glanced at the clock: 4:02.

I was too late. The recital had already started.

My mother came downstairs. I heard her walk up behind me, but I didn't turn around.

"Watching TV," she said. "Now *there's* a big waste of time on a Sunday afternoon."

"So?" I asked.

"*So,* I bet you could think of a hundred better, more productive things to do."

I hated the nagging sound of her words. I turned off the TV. "You're right," I told her. "And speaking of wasting time, why am I talking to you?" I got up off the couch and stomped down to my room.

"Stop, stop," I called over the music. "Time out."

I was practicing with Tomorrowland in my garage on Monday after school. I'd been in a terrible mood all day, and the way the band sounded wasn't helping. We were trying out the music for our new love song, but even with the cool sample from The Pretenders' "Don't Get Me Wrong" that Ryan had found, the song still sounded totally off.

"What's the matter now?" Kenny asked. I'd already stopped the band at least six times in the last twenty minutes.

"Does that sound good to *you?*" I shot back. "Can you really tell me you're happy with the way we sound?"

He scowled down at his keyboard. "No," he answered. "But we're trying to work it out. We'll get there if we keep jamming."

"Oh, right," I said. "Like another ten minutes of your useless blips are suddenly going to make us sound good?"

Kenny didn't look at me. He started running his finger slowly over his keys, obviously hurt.

I let out a sigh. "Sorry, man," I apologized. "Your part isn't useless—you know that. I'm just bugging today."

"Maybe we need to take ten minutes to collect ourselves," Jeff suggested.

"Jeff's right," I announced. "Take ten." I wandered over to the edge of the open garage door, staring out into my yard.

"You okay, Brad?" Jeff asked, stepping up beside me.

I kicked at the little tuft of grass growing

out of the seam where the garage met the driveway. "Yeah," I replied. "I'll be okay. Just give me a minute."

"Sure," Jeff said. "We count on you to stay cool, you know that."

"I know," I told him. "I just wish . . . I want us to pull the sound together so that we're as good as we should be. But I don't know how to do that."

"We'll figure it out," Jeff promised. "We'll be great. You'll see."

"Yeah," I said. "Okay." As I turned to go back inside, a green Honda pulled up the driveway. The car rattled to a stop, and I heard the yank of a parking brake.

Caitlin climbed out.

My jaw dropped. All I could see was her head poking over the top of the car. Her hair was down, glistening with auburn highlights in the afternoon sun. She wore a determined expression as she walked around the car and strode up the driveway.

Caitlin was just about the last person I wanted to see at that moment. My stomach sank. My guilty conscience twisted.

Worst of all, even with hurt written all over her face, Caitlin still looked beautiful. She was wearing a dark green dress that ended at her knees and a brown leather bomber jacket.

"Hello, Brad," she said.

"Hi," I said, looking down at the driveway.

"Why didn't you come?" she asked. "Yesterday you told me you'd be there."

"I couldn't make it," I said quickly. "I was going to go, but—"

"Don't lie to me," she said. "If you didn't want to come to my recital, why didn't you just say so?"

I leaned back against the garage doorway. "I *did* want to come," I protested. "I was all ready to go, but then I fell asleep and—"

Caitlin snorted. "Please," she told me. "At least do me the decency of thinking up a good lie. Is this how you get your jollies? You find some girl, be all nice to her, and then blow her off? You get her hopes all up, and—"

"Your hopes were up?"

Caitlin tightened her hands into fists. "Yes!" she snapped. "I was all excited, I told my sister, I told my parents you'd be there! I never felt so stupid in my whole life." Her bottom lip began to tremble.

"I . . . I just couldn't make it," I said.

"And now look at me," Caitlin mumbled. She pressed her lips together and squared her shoulders. Anger blazed in her eyes. "Coming here is the most pathetic thing I've ever done. I can't believe . . ."

"What?" I asked.

"I can't believe I was so excited about you," she said. She turned and ran toward her car.

I stared after her in stunned silence. Then I chased after her down the driveway. I caught up to her right before she opened her door. "Caitlin, wait," I gasped. "I'm sorry—"

She whirled on me. "Sorry, huh?" she spit out. "No, *I'm* sorry. I'm sorry that I fall for guys who don't have a shred of decency. I'm sorry I have a heart that keeps getting stepped on by guys too *scared* to admit they have feelings. That's it, right?"

I had no idea what to say.

Caitlin opened the car door. "Yeah," she said. "Have a nice life." She climbed into the car and slammed the door shut. I watched as she started the engine, threw the car in gear, and drove off down the street.

She hadn't even given me a chance to explain!

I turned back toward the house. The guys were standing a few feet up the driveway, staring at me solemnly. I'd almost forgotten they were there. They'd heard the whole thing.

"Wow," Kenny said. "That's one intense chick."

"Shut up, Kenny," I told him. I barged past them back into the garage. "Practice is over!" I shouted.

Four

THE NEXT DAY I hurried out of school the moment the final bell rang. I hadn't slept the night before, and the whole day at school I couldn't stop thinking about Caitlin.

As I strode through the Boulder High parking lot toward my blue '92 Jetta, I wondered what it was about her that was driving me so crazy. Her outburst yesterday had definitely blown me away. I'd never seen anything like that before. Or anyone like her. She was so . . . real. So honest. Not to mention beautiful. And she was all worked up over me! I'd never been the type to run after a girl, but I knew I'd never forgive myself if I didn't at least apologize to her.

Although I'd never been inside the September School, I knew where it was. The ride was too short for me to change my mind—and too long as far as my sweat-drenched palms were concerned. After I found a spot in their visitors' parking lot, I took a deep breath, climbed out of the car, and started toward the two-story, gray slate-covered building.

Just inside the front door I saw a girl with green-and-purple hair and a big black nose stud. She was running the water in a water fountain. Not drinking—just staring at the arc of water.

"Hey," I said. "Hi. Uh . . . you wouldn't happen to know a girl named—"

"Isn't it pretty?" the girl asked, still staring down at the fountain.

"Huh?"

"The water, the way it cascades. Water is a perfect form, a perfect element." She sighed happily.

"Uh, yeah," I replied. "Water's cool. Hey, listen. Do you know a girl named Caitlin Dawes?"

The girl blinked at me. The water in the fountain cut off abruptly. "Caitlin? That's the new cellist, right?"

I smiled. "Yeah, that's her. Do you know where I can find her?"

The girl thought about it for a moment. "I think I passed her in one of the music rooms. That was like ten minutes ago."

"Great," I said. "Where are the music rooms?"

She pointed behind her. "Go down the hall, hang a louie, up the stairs and straight on till sunset. You can't miss them. Just listen for the cacophony."

"Thanks," I told the girl. She was definitely weird, but who was I to judge? I left her staring at the fountain as I headed down the hall.

The hallway was pretty deserted, but I passed rooms with painters sitting on stools in front of easels and a busy sculpture studio. The walls were decorated with funky murals—all with a surprising amount of naked people in them. I took a left at the corner and hurried up the stairs.

I'd thought the girl was just being weird when she said "straight on till sunset," but at the end of the upstairs hall there was a giant painting of a beautiful sun dropping over the Rockies, with rich oranges, pinks, and purples bleeding down the walls of the hall. I headed toward the sunset, listening to the different types of music flooding from the practice spaces along the hallway. I heard a flute, a classical guitar, and a piano. I stopped short when I heard a cello.

The door was ajar. I peered through the little window.

Caitlin sat with her back to me. I could see

the edges of the cello between her knees, the top of its thick stem poking over her shoulder. I eased the door open and stepped inside.

She was deep in concentration—I didn't think she heard me enter. As quietly as I could, I sat down in a chair behind her.

She was playing a Bach suite—that much I recognized. I wasn't a *complete* idiot when it came to classical music. I admired her technique for a few moments. Her bow arm was graceful and strong, and she tilted her head as she reached for the low notes. It didn't take long to realize that Caitlin was good. Really good. She played slowly, savoring each note like she was riding on the music. I closed my eyes and let it wash over me.

It was beautiful, and it sounded . . . lonely. And sad. I'd never realized that a cello could sing with emotion. But the way Caitlin played was amazing.

Then she shifted, started playing harder, and an undercurrent of anger surged through her music with intense passion. Loneliness, sadness, anger . . . she was an incredible musician.

I felt swept away by her talent and beauty. This is what I'd missed the other day? I was such an idiot! I had to make it right.

Caitlin steered the song into a whisper of sad longing, then trailed off to a stop.

I opened my eyes. Lingering memories of the suite circled through my head as I stared at her back. Then I started to applaud.

Caitlin peered over her shoulder. When she saw me, she ducked her head and blushed. Then she gave a tired-sounding sigh. "Hi," she said.

I stood up and took a step toward her. "That was great," I told her. "I think I heard most of it. You're extremely talented."

"Thanks," she said. "The middle section still needs some tightening, but it's one of my favorite pieces."

"Bach, right?"

"You got it," she replied. "Cello Suite Number One."

"Well, I'm glad I got to hear it," I said. "It was insanely great. I'd love to hear you play again."

Caitlin exhaled—a sharp sniff. "I'm mad at you," she told me.

I took another step toward her. "For good reason," I admitted. "I should've been there. I was a jerk—"

"You were."

"I came here to apologize."

"Yeah, well . . ." Caitlin began practicing fingerings on the stem of her cello.

I moved closer, so close I could smell her.

She smelled nice, like . . . well, I don't know. She smelled sweet, comfortable.

"Listen," I said. "Let me make it up to you. Come out with me Friday—I'll take you out, just the two of us. It'll be special, I promise."

Her eyes opened wide with amused surprise. "You expect me to go out with you now?"

I smiled. "Well, not *now*. Friday. We'll have a great time."

"I don't know—"

I leaned over and looked in her eyes. "Yeah, you do. C'mon, I said I was sorry. And I meant it. You were right, I was a jerk. We'll start over, pretend like Sunday never happened."

Caitlin glanced away. She plucked a few strings and turned to look at me again. "Okay," she said. "Okay, sure. Yes."

I grinned. "Great," I told her. "Great. You won't regret giving me a second chance."

"I'd better not," she warned. But then she smiled too, that beautiful, radiant smile I'd thought I'd never see again.

It made me feel happier than I had in years.

Friday came around too quickly.

I barely had time to prepare. But by the time I picked Caitlin up at eight o'clock, I'd done laundry, showered, found something decent to wear, and made reservations at a cool restaurant that I knew was quiet enough so Caitlin and I could talk.

But once she was sitting next to me in my car, I suddenly felt shy. I'd been thinking about this date all week, making all the arrangements, but I'd forgotten to figure out something to talk about. When I'd imagined us together, I thought we'd chat easily, maybe about movies or something. But I hadn't expected her to look so good that it would make me tongue-tied.

Her hair fell in curls past her shoulders. She wore a dark blue dress made out of some velvety kind of material, with black leggings underneath. But it wasn't what she was wearing. Her very presence next to me made me feel nervous. Unsure.

We drove through the dark roads of Boulder, listening to Beck on the CD player. "How was your day today?" I asked, hoping I didn't sound nervous.

"Oh, great!" Caitlin responded. She seemed glad I'd broken the ice. "Well, actually, Becca and I had a fight."

"About what?"

"Oh, just stupid sister stuff. She's a year older than me, and she thinks she, like, owns the house. She wouldn't get out of the bathroom tonight for hours, even though I knew she was just making moony faces at herself in the mirror."

I chuckled. "You guys usually get along?"

"Yeah," Caitlin said. "We sort of respect each other's space, even though we're very different. She's not serious about much. And I'm not nearly as guy crazy as she is. But I love her to death, even if we have screaming matches."

"That's cool," I said.

Caitlin turned in her seat to face me. "How about you? Do you have any brothers or sisters?"

"Me?" I lowered the volume on the CD player. "No, I'm an only child."

"Huh," Caitlin said. "Do you ever wish you had brothers or sisters?"

"Sometimes," I admitted. "I used to want a brother . . . like when I was really little."

"Why a brother?"

I steered the car around a corner. "The usual reasons, I guess," I answered. "Someone to play with, someone who's always there—"

"Someone to talk to," Caitlin added.

"Yeah, that too."

"I guess it would have been nice to have a brother around when your parents—"

"Yeah," I interrupted, not wanting her to finish her sentence.

A heavy silence fell over us. I realized I'd been too abrupt. "Uh . . . ," I began, "I really wished—for a while anyway—that there was somebody else *between* me and my parents.

50

Like someone who was on my side, who knew what I was going through. Because for a while there my dealings with my parents got complicated."

"I think I know what you mean," Caitlin said. "We've moved a bunch of times, every time my father gets transferred. And without Becca there to sort of ground me, I probably would've gotten lost in all the changes. She's known me right from the beginning, which always helps me remember who I am."

I nodded. "Yeah, exactly," I told her. "I kind of didn't know where I belonged when my parents . . . split, uh, when my father moved out. You do get lost in the shuffle. And a brother would have . . ." I let my words trail away because all of a sudden I didn't want to talk about my parents anymore. "I don't know," I finished.

"I could see you with a brother," Caitlin said. "I can picture you two playing in your yard, football or whatever. I'll bet you were a cute little kid."

I didn't reply. I wasn't comfortable with this subject. And it was only going to get worse. The restaurant where I had reservations was right up ahead. Inside, we'd sit across from each other and it would be impossible to escape talking to her. I would have to keep having conversations like this, feeling uncomfortable like this.

So I changed my plans. Who wanted an intimate dinner anyway? With a sudden flash I knew exactly where to take her.

Five minutes later I pulled up in the parking lot of a club called Thunder Road. "Here we are," I announced, unbuckling my seat belt.

Caitlin looked confused. "I thought we were going out to eat," she said. "This isn't a restaurant, is it?"

"Nope," I said, climbing out of the car. "I'm not really hungry. And they usually have good music here. Do you mind?"

Caitlin got out, closed her door, and shrugged. "I guess not. Am I dressed okay for this place?"

"You look great," I told her.

The inside of Thunder Road was dark, smoky, and noisy. I paid for us to get in, and the door guy attached underage-ID bracelets to our wrists. I led Caitlin through the crowd to where we could get a good view of the stage. Onstage was a basic rock band—a guitarist, a drummer, a bassist, a singer—playing generic bar rock. But they were *loud,* that was the important thing.

"Brad!" Caitlin shouted into my ear over the ringing music. "There's an open table over there!"

"What?" I shouted back.

"An open table! Can we sit?"

I nodded and headed over to a small, battered table by the wall at the edge of the crowd.

Perfect, I thought. I had a beautiful date by my side. We were in a club, listening to music—which was as cool a date as anyone could ask for. Who needed a romantic, quiet dinner? This was fun and exciting.

"Can we get a drink?" Caitlin shouted into my ear.

"What?"

"A drink! A Coke!"

"Oh, sure!" I hollered back. The music was deafening—in fact, the main speaker was right above our heads.

I flagged down a tired-looking waitress in a tight black T-shirt. She nodded that she'd seen me, picked up a few half-finished beers off an abandoned nearby table, placed them on her tray, and headed our way. "What'll it be?" she yelled, her breath reeking of cigarette smoke.

"A Coke and a Dr Pepper!" I shouted, showing her my underage wristband.

The waitress nodded again and turned away. As she stepped toward the bar two drunken guys collided with her. Her tray teetered. The half-empty beers slid off the edge. For a long, frozen moment I watched the beers hover in space. Then they crash-landed on our table, spewing beer all over Caitlin's velvet dress.

Caitlin sat up straight, her arms straight out at her sides. I had to give her credit—she didn't freak out or anything like most girls would have. She just closed her eyes for a second and shook her head.

The waitress handed her a pile of napkins and kind of shrugged before heading off to the bar.

"You okay?" I yelled at Caitlin.

She rolled her eyes while patting at her dress with the napkins. "I've been better!" she screamed.

"What?"

"I'm fine!"

I nodded and turned my attention toward the band onstage. They seemed to be finishing up their song with a long guitar solo.

After Caitlin had sopped up the beer in her lap as best she could, she dumped the damp napkins on the table. "So!" she shouted at me. "Is this where you take all your dates?"

"Sorry! What?"

"Do you come here a lot?"

"Say it again!"

"Do you come here a lot!"

"Oh, no!" I replied. "This is like my third time here ever!" My throat was already starting to get a little sore from screaming. But the pain was worth it if I got through this date with Caitlin in one piece.

"Brad, aiwa togo omay!"

I wondered stupidly for a second if she was speaking Japanese. "What?"

"Aiwa togo omay!" she shouted again.

"Sorry!" I yelled. "One more time!"

"I want to go home!" Caitlin shouted at the top of her lungs—at the same exact second the music onstage cut off. Everyone in the club turned to look at her. She closed her eyes and shook her head again.

"You want to go home," I repeated.

"Yes," Caitlin whispered.

"But we just got here." People were standing around, looking at us and laughing.

She glared at me. "Brad," she said. "I want to leave. Now. Should I call Becca to come get me, or will you drive me home?"

"Fine," I said shortly. "Let's go."

We stood up just as the waitress returned with our drinks. I paid her for the sodas we didn't even get to drink and followed Caitlin out of the club.

Caitlin climbed into my car without a word. She was still pretty wet from the beer, and the expression on her face was both miserable and angry. We drove in silence all the way to her house.

As I pulled to a stop in her driveway she turned to face me. "Brad," she asked, "why did you take me to that club? That was an awful first date."

"You're mad at me," I said. "I guess you have a right to be, with the beer and everything."

She groaned. "I'm not mad, just frustrated. And not because of the beer—although that wasn't the highlight of the evening. Why did you take me there?"

"I don't know," I replied. "I just thought it would be fun."

"Was that where you were planning to take me? It took a lot longer getting there than it did coming back. Like it wasn't your original destination."

I thought about how to answer. "I guess not," I admitted. Once I started telling the truth, it all came out more easily. "I was going to take you to a cool restaurant, but—"

"But what? Why'd you change your mind?" Caitlin looked hurt. "Didn't you want to get to know me, in a place where we could talk?"

"Uh, sure. I want to get to know you," I assured her.

"Then *what?*" Caitlin demanded.

I turned to look into her eyes. Which wasn't the best idea. I glanced away. But not quick enough.

"Aha," she said. "You didn't want *me* to get to know *you.*"

I gripped the steering wheel. "Maybe," I said.

"Why?" she asked. "What have you got to hide?"

"Nothing, really, I guess. It's just . . ." I turned my whole body to face her. "You do this thing when we get talking, you bring out all these feelings in me. . . ." My explanation was starting to sound stupid. What *was* I afraid of?

"They're not good emotions," I tried to explain. "Not the usual date emotions, which would be fine. But other stuff. Things I don't want to think about. You're always asking me questions about stuff that's too personal."

"Oh," Caitlin whispered. "So you took me someplace we couldn't talk."

"Yeah."

Caitlin shifted in her seat. "My mother tells me that I dig into people too much," she said. "That I expect everyone to be as open as I am. Sorry about that. So what's off-limits to talk about?"

"My parents' divorce, for one," I told her.

"All right," she said.

But then I felt the strangest sensation—I felt sad. Not because of the divorce. But because Caitlin couldn't ask me about it. It seemed wrong to put limits on our conversations. "You know what?" I said. "You ask me whatever you want. It's not your fault. But don't be surprised if I can't answer sometimes."

57

Caitlin laughed. "You're a complicated guy, Brad Myers," she told me. She ducked her head and peered out the car window before turning back to face me. "Listen," she said. "It's too late to salvage this date, but next time *I* get to pick the place, okay?"

I smiled. "Okay. Cool."

"Great." She opened the car door and slid out. For a second she stood on the edge of her driveway. Then she stuck her head back into the car and put her palm against my cheek. "I really do like you, you know," she whispered, rubbing her thumb against my lips. "Luckily for you, I like guys who are quiet, deep, complicated . . . and difficult to get to know."

I swallowed. "I like you too," I told her. "Really."

She pulled back her hand. "Call me soon, okay?"

"I will. I promise."

Caitlin closed the car door. I watched as she climbed up the driveway and disappeared inside the house.

All things considered, it had been an excellent first date.

Five

"SUNDAY," CAITLIN SAID. "And I've decided what we're doing."

I'd talked to Caitlin on the phone almost every night for a week, but we'd both been too busy to get together in person. I couldn't wait to see her again. Our conversations had been fun—no heavy talks about our parents or anything, which was fine with me. Mostly we chatted about our days, about the new friends Caitlin was making at school, and what we were up to with our music. Nice, long talks, where we made each other laugh.

"Okay," I said. "Where are we going?"

"Well, I read that there was a glacier still up in the mountains, left over from the Ice Age. Saint Mary's Glacier. Have you been there?"

"Nope."

"I've never seen a glacier before. Want to go?"

"Definitely," I replied. "The mountains are always cool with me. Sometimes I forget they're there."

Caitlin laughed. "How do you forget mountains?"

"It's easy when you live in Boulder all your life," I told her.

"Well, you and I will have such an amazing time in the mountains that you'll never forget them again," Caitlin promised.

I totally believed her.

On Sunday, Caitlin arrived while I was still eating breakfast. We had to take her car because I didn't trust mine to make the uphill trek.

I led Caitlin into the kitchen, where my mother was eating a bowl of cereal at the table. I felt a little weird introducing them since my mother hadn't even known that Caitlin existed.

"Mom, this is Caitlin," I said quickly. "We're going for a drive in the mountains today."

My mother raised an eyebrow and nodded hello.

"Good to meet you, Mrs. Myers," Caitlin said.

"Brad's the only Myers around here," she

told Caitlin. "I'm Ms. Sullivan." That was her maiden name.

"Well, good to meet you, Ms. Sullivan, then," Caitlin amended cheerfully.

I hovered behind Caitlin, feeling nervous and awkward. My mother was checking Caitlin out, and I knew she'd give me a hard time later if she didn't like her. The possibilities for embarrassing disaster were heavy-duty.

"Would you like some breakfast?" my mother asked.

"Oh, no thanks," Caitlin replied. "I ate at home."

I slung my jacket over my arm and grabbed a pair of gloves. Then I glanced over at Caitlin. She had on a windbreaker, without gloves or a scarf.

"I don't think you'll be warm enough," I told her.

Caitlin glanced down at her outfit. "Oh," she said in dismay. "It's colder up in the mountains, isn't it? I totally forgot about that. Um . . . I don't really have a winter coat yet."

"Caitlin's from California," I explained to my mother.

"Oh, yes?" Mom pursed her lips at Caitlin in sort of a frown.

I braced myself.

My mother stood up and wiped her mouth with a napkin. "I'm sure my winter things will fit you," she told Caitlin. "Let's see what we've got."

I stared after Caitlin as she followed Mom down the hall toward the coat closet. The last thing I'd expected was for my mother to be all *nice*.

I grabbed my backpack and began filling it with grape juice boxes and chewy granola bars for the trip. I also stuck in a map just in case. The roads up through the mountains were pretty simple, but you never could tell when a shortcut or something would come in handy.

Caitlin and my mother came back into the kitchen, with Caitlin carrying Mom's long wool overcoat, a brown hat, and gloves. They were talking about San Diego.

"So you don't miss it?" my mother asked.

"Not at all," Caitlin assured her. "I like Boulder, and San Diego was too . . . um—"

"Conservative?"

Caitlin nodded. "How'd you know?"

My mother smiled. "After Colorado Springs it's probably the most conservative city in America. There's a navy training base there, after all. My father was in the navy, and I spent my childhood moving from base to base. I know how conservative the military can be."

"A navy brat," Caitlin said.

Mom chuckled and nodded.

I cleared my throat. "We should go," I

told Caitlin. I wasn't eager for them to keep talking. There was something deeply creepy about my mother and Caitlin getting along.

"Okay," Caitlin said, favoring me with a smile. Then she turned back to my mother. "I'm glad to have met you, Ms. Sullivan."

"Keep warm now," Mom instructed Caitlin gruffly. She tilted her head toward me. "And don't let him get to you," she continued conspiratorially. "His bark is worse than his bite."

"Mom," I groaned. "Enough."

Then Caitlin reached out and grabbed my mother's hand. The hair rose on the back of my neck as I saw a look of alarm cross Mom's face.

"Ms. Sullivan," Caitlin murmured, "I really hope we can talk a lot more in the future."

I didn't! What on earth was she saying? "Time to go!" I called, but neither of them noticed me. My mother stared at Caitlin with an odd, confused look in her eyes. Then she yanked her hand out of Caitlin's grasp.

I grabbed Caitlin's arm. "Let's go," I whispered urgently.

Caitlin turned to me. "Okay," she said. She smiled at my mother and started to follow me out of the kitchen.

My mother shook her head and followed us

to the front door. Just as we stepped out onto the front porch she said to me, "Brad, can I talk to you for a moment?"

I was about to say no, that we had to get going, but Caitlin then said, "I'll wait in the car." Before I could protest, Caitlin was headed down the driveway and my mom had begun her little speech.

"Brad," she said, "you know I don't approve of a Sunday road trip. This is your junior year—the most important for your college applications. You should be spending this time studying—"

"Mom," I interrupted. "Chill. I'll be back in plenty of time for homework, I promise."

She opened her mouth as though she wanted to argue but didn't say anything. "All right," she conceded. "Just don't make a habit of this type of thing." Then she turned and went back inside, closing the door behind her.

"What was that about?" Caitlin asked as I climbed into her Honda.

I was beyond frustrated with my mother. But one look at Caitlin and I forgot all my anger. There was no way I was going to let my mother's nagging ruin today. No way. "She was just bugging me about homework. No big deal."

"Oh." Caitlin turned the key in the ignition. "Well, are we ready to go?"

"You know what, Caitlin?" I smiled at her, brushing a strand of her long hair away from her face. "I've never been more ready."

A few minutes later we were on the road heading west, into the thick of the Rocky Mountains.

Sarah McLaughlin's "Building a Mystery" filled the car. We listened silently for a moment, then Caitlin began to sing along. She didn't have a very strong voice, but it was sweet and in tune, and I stayed quiet for a while, listening, before I joined in. As walls of craggy red rock started to appear along the sides of the highway we both whisper-sang a bunch of songs together.

There's always something cool about singing with someone, especially in a car. I felt relaxed and peaceful with Caitlin. I didn't even feel like showing off my voice, which I usually do to impress girls.

The sunlight streaming in through the windows made the car feel warm and cozy, even though it was getting chillier outside as we rose in altitude. The rocky foothills loomed up on either side of the road, with scrubby brush and bristly evergreens dotting the hillsides. It doesn't take long to get back to nature in Colorado—it's always right around the corner.

As we coasted down a short valley I reached

out and closed my hand over Caitlin's on the gearshift. She intertwined her fingers with mine. Her hand felt warm and soft in my own.

She turned to smile at me. "You know," she said, "I really liked your mom. And she's very beautiful. I can see where you get your looks from."

"Huh," I said with a big, stupid grin. Caitlin thought I was good-looking!

But then something about the way Caitlin had complimented my mother bothered me. I didn't want Caitlin thinking that my mom was this great woman—especially when my mom and I barely had a speaking relationship.

I dropped Caitlin's hand as she shifted to a lower gear for a steep incline in the road. "My mom's okay," I said. "But she kind of drives me crazy. She's always harping about my schoolwork. And I do fine. I mean, it's not like I'm messing up in school or anything—I don't know what her deal is."

"Maybe it's just her way of reaching out to you."

"I don't know."

Caitlin shrugged. "That's just the feeling I get," she said. "Like she doesn't know how to talk to you, so she says critical things instead. It's the same for my mother and me some-times."

"Maybe," I replied. That was enough talk

about my mom. "So . . . ," I began, changing the subject, "what are you going to do when we get to this glacier?"

Caitlin giggled. "Make snow cones, of course."

"Great," I said with a laugh. "I brought grape juice, so grape snow cones it is."

"My favorite flavor."

I took Caitlin's hand again as the view outside became slowly more sweeping, jagged, and beautiful.

An hour or so later we crested a steep incline on a road carved right into the mountain, protected from the cliff's edge by only a flimsy-looking wooden railing. And suddenly the misty, majestic panorama of the Continental Divide was spread out before us.

"*Oh,*" Caitlin murmured softly in awe. I was in complete agreement with her.

"This is the Continental Divide. We can stop," I said, pointing to a man-made scenic view station on the side of the road. Caitlin pulled over, and we both got out of the car.

I always forget what the Rockies actually look like. They're so truly vast that it's hard to keep them in your mind when they aren't in front of you. They're almost too big for your brain to hold. Pictures don't do them justice because when you actually look at them, you see more than just one part. Your eye goes from an impossibly giant hunk of mountain, to a sheer rock wall, to a broad, patchy expanse of green trees, to a snow-covered peak that scratches the sky, to a stomach-droppingly deep valley with puffy white clouds floating by *below* you, all at once.

"It's . . . amazing," Caitlin said, resting her chin on my shoulder. "Wow."

I knew exactly what she meant. The mountains always made me feel small and insignificant but also amazingly alive at the same time.

"Why's it called 'The Continental Divide'?" she asked.

"Um," I began, trying to remember what we'd been taught in school. "Uh . . . this is where the main rivers from the north separate, um, *diverge*. From right here, rivers flow to the east and the west in different directions. All the water, like, flows downstream from here, both ways." I paused for a second. "I think that's why anyway."

"I like that," Caitlin said. "Where we're standing right now, that's where the rivers come together."

"Or separate."

"Well, yeah," she replied. "You can think that if you want, Mr. Half Empty. But I prefer to think of the rivers coming together, right here, right in front of us." She put her arm around my waist. "Just like us."

"Okay," I said, squeezing her gently. "Just like us. For us the Continental Divide will reverse the flow of its rivers."

Caitlin nodded. "You'd better believe it," she whispered.

I believed it.

A few hours later we finally reached the rough parking lot for the hiking trail up to Saint Mary's Glacier. There were a few other tourists milling about, and the lot was about two-thirds full.

Caitlin parked, and we both pulled on our extra winter accessories. As I climbed out of the car and took a deep breath of the crisp, clean air I noticed how cute Caitlin looked in my mother's old brown hat. It was a simple woolen cap, but Caitlin pulled down its brim so it looked retro seventies. On second thought, I realized that it wasn't retro *anything*. The hat probably was left over from the seventies. My mother never threw anything away.

"Ready?" I asked.

"Sure," Caitlin replied. And she smiled her devastating smile.

The hike up the dirt path wasn't too steep—we even passed an old couple on their way down. We were below the snow line, although white-capped mountains rose up in the distance. I spotted a tiny rose quartz crystal by a shelf of exposed rock and picked it up. "For you," I said, handing it to Caitlin. "My friend Kenny says rose quartz is good for the emotions. I don't know if that's true, but it's pretty anyway."

"It's beautiful," Caitlin said, tucking the stone in her pocket.

We kept walking, glove in glove. Around one rocky corner we found a mirror-perfect mountain lake. Then we climbed past a scrub grass-covered outcropping and came face-to-face with the glacier.

The glacier wasn't a giant wall of ice like you might expect, but it was still pretty big. It looked like a huge frozen river, pouring over a passage in the mountain above it, cascading downward, trailing off into a broad plain surrounded by chunks of rocks and pebbles.

"Race you!" I called.

"You're on!" Caitlin shouted. She grabbed the sleeve of my coat and pulled me back, knocking me off balance as she ran ahead.

"Cheater!" I yelled after her, and I took off running to catch up, my backpack bouncing against my shoulders.

Caitlin won, but she had that unfair head start. We both collapsed against the glacier and gasped for breath, laughing. I was able to get my breathing back to normal much faster than Caitlin was. She sucked in deep gusts of air, holding her sides.

"It's the altitude," I explained. "You're not used to it."

"I'm . . . okay," she gasped in return.

"So," I told her, grinning widely. "You got to touch a glacier."

She nodded, wincing a little. "Yeah," she breathed, running her hand over the weird ropy twists in the ice. "It feels cool. We sure didn't have . . . anything like this . . . in San Diego."

"I bet."

We hung out by the glacier for a while, drinking the juice and eating the granola bars. There was no need to talk with such gorgeous surroundings. And sitting in silence with Caitlin was better than any conversation I'd ever had with other girls.

After a little while, though, I noticed that she kept pressing her lips together and blinking.

"Are you okay?" I asked.

Caitlin shook her head, wincing. "I don't know," she told me. "I have a killer headache, right here." She touched a spot below the crown of her head, right underneath the edge of her hat in back. "A sharp, shooting pain. It's really awful."

"I'm sure it's the altitude again," I said, trying to reassure her. "People from lower altitudes almost always get headaches around here from not getting enough oxygen to the brain. You'll get used to it in a few months or maybe less."

"Yeah, that must be it." Caitlin massaged her neck. "I've gotten them in Boulder too, like migraines. They started pretty much when I first moved to Colorado."

"You'll get used to it," I repeated. "You okay to walk back to the car?"

"I'll be fine," Caitlin said firmly. "But . . ."

"What?"

"Would it be okay if you drove home? I don't think I'm up to that."

The headache must have been worse than she was letting on. "Are you sure you'll be all right?" I asked.

"Yeah," Caitlin said. "Don't worry about it."

But something in her eyes told me I *should* worry.

After a few hours on the road I could tell Caitlin was feeling better. She rested her head against my shoulder as I drove.

Darkness fell early. Guiding the car down the dark, curvy roads with Caitlin leaning against me and music softly filtering from the radio felt perfect, a time I knew I would always remember. I was so happy that I actually started to feel a little dazed—a little out of it. So I rolled down the window a notch to get some fresh air.

And almost immediately smelled a familiar clean, icy, thick scent.

"It's going to snow," I told Caitlin.

"How can you tell?" she murmured.

"I can smell it," I replied. "When you've grown up in Colorado, you can always recognize the smell of snow."

She sat up straight. "I've never seen snow falling," she said, peering out the window. There was an edge of excitement in her voice.

"Never?"

"Well, on TV and in the movies," she said. "But never in real life."

"Snow gets old fast," I warned her. "Mostly it's just cold and wet. Especially when you have to shovel it, you get sick of winter pretty quickly."

"Not me," she said. "I can't wait."

Just then I noticed the first flurries drifting down in the light from a street lamp. "Hang on," I told her. I pulled over to the side of the road beside the next street lamp I spotted.

"We're stopping?"

"Yeah," I said. "C'mon."

I'd parked on a low shoulder beside a weathered wooden fence. Beyond the fence a grassy field stretched out into the distance. I could just make out a few dark dots of cattle on the horizon. I took Caitlin's hand and led her under the lamppost. "Look up," I instructed.

From high above in the blue-gray sky the snow fell in patternless chaos down through the yellow light.

"Oh, it's lovely," Caitlin whispered.

I stared at her as she continued to look upward. Snowflakes had caught in her long eyelashes and rested on her cheeks. I swallowed hard. She was the most beautiful sight I'd ever witnessed.

"Open your mouth," I told her. "Catch them on your tongue."

She did, smiling as snowflakes landed on her pink tongue. "Delicious," she murmured.

I had to touch her. I took her in my arms, twirling her in the cold, serene snowfall. She laughed as we slowly spun.

Now. The right moment was now. To do what I'd wanted to do from the first second I'd met her. I didn't feel a single tinge of fear or uncertainty. I'd never felt more sure of anything in my entire life.

I stopped suddenly, holding her face-to-face in my arms. She looked confused for a second but then smiled shyly and closed her eyes.

While downy snowflakes sifted around us in a perfect field of pure white, I kissed her.

And it was magic.

Six

"I WILL NEVER tear us apart . . . ," I sang, humming the rest of the melody as the hot water pelted my skin. Then I cut myself off, nearly dropping the soap in surprise. Usually I ended up spending my morning shower singing the song that woke me up on my alarm clock. But I'd never heard the song I was humming this morning.

I'd made it up.

Quickly I hopped out of the shower and began toweling off, trying to remember the melody in my head. To my surprise, it stayed fixed in place, as easy to recall as my own name. And it was good, I was sure of that.

I hummed the melody over and over as I got dressed, and I had no trouble thinking of a funky rhythm that could back up the tune and expand on it. Then a churning melodic section that could propel the song popped into my head and even a cool bass line! That had never happened to me. Usually I labored endlessly trying to put a song together. *Never* had one just appeared in my brain.

Dropping the shirt I was about to put on, I scrambled to find a pen. The words flew onto the page.

> I will never tear us apart.
> You are my heart.
> Though there are separate ways to flow to the sea,
> we will flow together, you and me—
> or stay right where we felt most alive—
> balancing on the brink of the Continental Divide.

After I'd scribbled those lyrics down, I stared at them in wonder. This was exactly what I'd been searching for. It wasn't perfect yet, but the lyrics were meaningful, the guys in Tomorrowland would dig the basis of the music, and it was about love. . . .

I froze. I couldn't show these lyrics to anyone, could I? They were too cheesy, too revealing, too *embarrassing!* The words made it so obvious what I felt for Caitlin. What if she didn't feel the same way? Or what if we didn't last together? After all, we'd only had two dates.

If I showed everyone those lyrics and then Caitlin and I broke up, I'd be setting myself up for horrible pain. And worse—public pain. Was it a risk worth taking?

All day in school I thought about it. I didn't pay attention in any of my classes. Instead I continually pulled the lyrics out of my notebook and stared at them.

The line "I will never tear us apart" worried me the most. That was a promise, a promise I didn't know if I could keep. Sure, I felt that way now, but hadn't I learned that love doesn't always last? My parents had probably felt this strongly for each other when they first met. I'd watched their love disappear, and they'd even made *marriage* vows. What if my attraction to Caitlin was just raging hormones or something?

No. It was more than that.

How could I describe what I felt? It was too soon to call it *love*, but I couldn't think of another word. When I thought of Caitlin, thought of her warm lips against mine . . . I thought *love*.

And, I rationalized, *I do feel it right now, and songs are about what's going on right now. They don't have to be about forever . . . they can capture a moment in time.*

Sitting in math, I let out a heavy sigh. I was supposed to be the cold, rational one. What would the guys say when I whipped out a mushy love song? But still, I couldn't deny I had just written the best song of my life, for Caitlin.

After school I sat quietly on my father's abandoned workbench, watching the guys set up their instruments in my garage. I had the lyric sheet folded up in my back pocket.

"Hey, Brad-man," Kenny called. "You joining us today or what?"

"I'm here," I replied, sliding off the workbench. I took a deep breath. "Jeff, I want to show you something."

Jeff slouched over to me. "What?"

Jeff was a good test subject. If he laughed or thought the lyrics were stupid, I could always pretend I'd written them as a joke. I dug the sheet out of my pocket and passed it to him. "Here," I said. "We wanted to do songs about love."

Jeff unfolded the paper and began to read. He stared at the lyrics *forever*. I started to feel nervous. "It's just an idea," I said quickly. "No biggie."

He glanced up at me. "These are *great*," he said, his voice tinged with excitement.

"Really?" I asked. "You really think so?"

"Absolutely. No question. *Continental Divide*—I *love* that."

"I was thinking of that for the title," I admitted.

"What's that?" Ryan called to us. "What are you guys up to? Telling secrets?"

"No secret," Jeff replied. "Just our new song."

"Yeah?" Kenny said. "Let's hear it."

Jeff read the lyrics. It was the first time I'd heard them out loud, and I had to say, they *were* pretty decent.

"Cool," Kenny said when Jeff finished. "You got a tune to go with that?"

"Absolutely." I headed over to my keyboard and began punching out the melody I'd first hummed in the shower. "You see how that works?" I asked. "This could be rhythmic background. . . ."

The guys all picked up on their parts enthusiastically. Andre added a flourish to the bass line that I never would've dreamed up, but it made the song better. Jeff's drumming was basic but solid—a classic heartbeat rhythm. But Kenny thought up the best twist of all.

"You know what?" he asked thoughtfully. *"Didgeridoo."*

"There's no need to get rude," I replied playfully. I was feeling good.

"No, no," Kenny protested. "A didgeridoo is an Australian instrument, kind of like a long pipe. It makes this cool rumbling noise that always reminds me of mountains, or at least rolling hills. It'll fill in the background in the most righteous way."

"Excellent," Andre muttered.

Hearing praise from Andre gave me goose bumps. I couldn't help grinning.

"Any sample suggestions?" Ryan asked.

"Well, didn't you want to drop in a sample of Beth's voice or something?" I answered. "But other than that, you're on your own. Play with the love thing."

Ryan nodded. I could *see* the wheels in his brain already churning through his endless catalog of computerized samples. He would definitely come up with something amazing, I was sure.

Tomorrowland was on a major roll. I'd never felt us working together more cohesively, like all the parts were just clicking into place. It was a pure rush.

During a rest Jeff sat up straight, a big smile on his face. "You know what this is?" he asked.

"What?" Ryan replied.

Jeff slapped his leg. "This here is a bona fide *breakthrough!*" he cheered.

"Right on," Andre added.

Jeff turned to me. "You know what, Bradman?"

"No, I don't know *what*, Jeff-dude," I responded with a laugh. "But you're going to tell me, no?"

Jeff snorted happily. "I just totally had a good feeling about that Caitlin girl," he said. "Right from the moment she first freaked out and yelled at you. Right then and there I thought, *She's going to blow Brad's mind.* Talk about a good influence!"

Here it comes, I thought. *I should have known they'd make fun of me.* But somehow I didn't feel embarrassed like I'd expected. I just felt like grinning. And I did, so widely my cheeks began to hurt. "You were right," I told him. "You were so right."

"How'd your rehearsal go yesterday?" Caitlin asked, coming out of my kitchen with a glass of orange juice. It was a Tuesday after school, and Caitlin and I had my house all to ourselves. We often did on weeknights since my mom worked late so much. Which, of course, was just fine with me.

I smiled up at her from the living-room couch. This was my favorite time with Caitlin. We did all the normal boyfriend-girlfriend stuff—going to the movies, talking on the phone, going out to dinner—but afternoons like this, our downtime together, just hanging out, was the best.

"It was incredible." Taking her hand, I pulled her down next to me.

"Watch it!" She giggled, struggling to maintain a hold on her glass. "I'll spill!" She carefully set her orange juice down on the coffee table. "Okay. Now tell me all about it."

I leaned back on the couch, thinking about our rehearsal the day before. It had been a blast—a totally psyched-up jamming and dancing free-for-all. For the past couple of weeks, ever since "Continental Divide," all five of us had been pumping out completely original, rocking songs and song fragments. We were in the zone. It was like we could do no wrong.

"It was awesome," I told Caitlin. "I'm telling you—we're riding a creative rocket or something."

She squeezed my hand. "I'm so happy for you guys. You deserve it."

I knew Caitlin meant every word one hundred percent. "Thanks." I reached over and pulled her into my arms, her head tucked under my chin. We were silent for a minute, just enjoying how it felt to sit together so closely. I kissed the top of her head, inhaling the light berry smell of her hair.

After a moment she pulled away. "Brad?"

"Yeah?"

"When do you think I can come to one of your rehearsals?"

"Not yet," I told her. "But soon."

She sat up straight. "Soon?"

I nodded.

"You promise?" she asked, raising one eyebrow.

"Definitely." I grabbed her hand and squeezed it. "We just want to perfect our songs a bit more before other people hear us."

"Well, okay," Caitlin responded. "But you better stick to your promise. Because I'm telling you, Beth and I are starting to wonder if you make these rehearsal sessions up to get away from us or something."

I laughed, leaning in to give Caitlin a kiss. She and Beth, Ryan's girlfriend, had become friends over the past couple of weeks, and the two of them were dying to come hear us play. "Trust me," I told her, cupping her head in my hands. "The last thing I ever want is to get away from you."

In December, Caitlin and I decided to go skiing in Vail. She'd never been skiing before, but since Vail was just two hours away and I'd been going every winter since I was six years old, I figured I could teach her the fundamentals. And she was athletic enough—Caitlin probably could have punched me out if she'd wanted to, no problem.

We drove up to Vail in my tuned-up Jetta.

When we arrived at the ski resort, I helped Caitlin rent skis and boots (I had my own), and we bought lift tickets.

"We can start on the bunny hill," I told her after we were fully outfitted. "But it might be better if you just threw yourself into it and avoided all the kiddies."

"I don't know," Caitlin replied, furrowing her brow. "What if I stink?"

I steered her toward the chairlift that led to the top of an easy intermediate hill. "I've never seen you stink at *anything* you try to do," I countered as we got in line, "so why would that happen with skiing?"

"Because I've never done it before!"

"You'll be fine," I promised.

As we waited, Caitlin stared up at the chairlifts warily. "Now how do I get on this thing?" she asked.

"It's easy," I told her, massaging her shoulders through her yellow parka. "You just bend your knees and let the gondola sweep you up."

"Just like that?" she asked, looking worried.

I nodded. "Just like that. Piece of cake."

"I don't know . . . ," she mumbled as we moved forward.

But when it was our turn, Caitlin didn't hesitate to shuffle into place. We were airborne in seconds. The chilly wind rushed through my hair as we traveled up the mountain, dangling in space.

"Wow! This is so pretty!" Caitlin exclaimed. Her eyes were sparkling with excitement, and her cheeks were red from the cold.

"It's the best," I said. I pointed down at the route through the trees. "See that? That's the ski trail. See the skiers?"

She nodded as she watched the skiers glide by underneath us. "That looks like so much fun!"

I grinned. I knew she'd get psyched once she saw the slopes.

But her tune changed when we got closer to the end of the line.

"Uh . . . I'm not sure about this," Caitlin muttered when the landing area came into view. "I don't even know how to steer!"

"Do you know how to skate?"

"*Roller* skate."

"That's fine," I said. "It's nearly the same thing. Just imagine you have long, flat roller skates on your feet."

"What are these *poles* for?" she demanded, raising one into the air. "There aren't any poles in roller skating!"

"They're for balance," I explained, "and for getting back on your feet if you fall. Just tuck them under your arms as you go down the hill."

Caitlin sighed. "Do I jump off this thing when we reach the top or what?"

"A little jump is good," I told her. "Push yourself off the gondola and slide forward until you're out of the way."

We were right up to the landing area.

"Okay," Caitlin announced. "Here goes nothing!"

We landed with no problem. Caitlin glided ahead like a pro, and I followed right behind her. She became a little wobbly when she tried to make the left toward the top of the slope, but she straightened out right away.

"I think I'm getting the hang of this," she said, sounding surprised. "And I get the feeling that you can go *fast* on these."

I paused beside her at the start of the downhill run. "You'll be great," I assured her. "And yeah, you can go fast. *Really* fast. But I'd start more slowly if I were you, going side to side at first—"

Before I could finish my sentence, Caitlin inhaled a deep breath and launched herself down the slope. She took off like a bullet.

"Side to side!" I screamed. "Slalom! *Slalom!*"

Then I realized that even if she could hear me, she'd have no idea what I was talking about. I zipped off after her.

Caitlin crouched down in the classic racing

position, which she must have seen on TV or something. And she was picking up speed way too fast.

I followed as quickly as I could, but I was afraid that if I bombed down like she was doing, I would completely lose control and wipe out. And there was always the small matter of the trees. . . . It's hard to *steer* when you're zooming headlong.

A thin shriek escaped from Caitlin as she headed toward two other skiers in front of her. I was starting to feel scared. Skiing accidents were nasty—she could break a leg . . . or worse. My stomach dropped as I struggled desperately to catch up. I didn't even want to think about what could happen.

"Out of my way!" Caitlin hollered at the two guys ahead of her. *"Out of control!"*

The guys dove off to the sides, tumbling into the snow as she shot safely between them.

"Sorry!" I called out to the two poor guys, now covered in white powder, as I passed them.

"Snow bunnies," the guy on the left grunted in disgust.

Up ahead Caitlin was heading directly for a bunch of trees. She looked like she was trying to turn but couldn't quite figure out how.

"Left! Left!" I yelled. "Lean *left!*" But my

screams did absolutely no good. She continued to streak toward the trees in a blur.

Just as I was sure she was going to wipe out in the most horrible way imaginable, Caitlin hit a small turn ramp with a sharp stop. She tilted dangerously to the side for a second, then straightened out, careening just past the edge of the trees, missing them entirely.

I sighed with relief as I continued to chase her. She was almost to the bottom.

But then a horrible thought struck me. *How is she going to stop?*

"Just sit down!" I hollered down the slope. *"Sit down!"*

Either Caitlin didn't hear me or didn't understand what I was yelling because she shot past the normal stopping point at the bottom of the hill . . . and headed right toward a snow-covered drainage ditch.

"That lady's going in the *ditch!*" some little kid shouted to the left of me, and sure enough, Caitlin plowed over the edge of the small ravine, disappearing from view. A small cloud of snow erupted from the place into which she had vanished.

I swung toward the ditch, my heart thumping in my chest. If she was hurt, I would never forgive myself. I should've made sure that she knew the safety rules of skiing, that she knew how to turn, that she at least knew how to snowplow. It was all my fault. If she was hurt . . .

I couldn't allow myself to finish that thought.

About a yard away from the ditch I lost momentum, so I detached from my skis and clomped over in my boots as fast as I could. I peered over the edge.

And saw Caitlin facedown in the snow.

She wasn't moving. Her skis had come free on either side of her, and her poles were sprawled a few feet away.

I jumped into the ditch, sinking past my calves in the snow. *Please let her be all right,* I prayed as I waded toward her. *Please . . .*

Only when I put my hand on her back did I realize that her face was turned to the side . . . and that she was *laughing.*

I flipped her over. "Oh, wow," I said, gasping with relief. "You're okay. I was so worried, you don't know—"

That brought on another burst of laughter. "Oh, Brad," she choked out, wiping snow away from her face with a mitten, "that was the *best.* Let's do it again!"

"Are you *insane?*" I thundered, suddenly feeling angry as my worry ebbed away. "Do you know what could've happened to you? Do you?"

Caitlin's laughter stopped abruptly. "Yeah,

I know," she told me. "But I'm fine. I had fun. Now I know what all the fuss about skiing is for."

I sat back in the snow, shaking my head.

Caitlin whacked me playfully on the shoulder with her mitten. "Relax, Brad," she scolded me. "I'm fine, really. I wasn't as out of control as I seemed. I knew I could just sit down at any time—I was never going too fast for that. I'm okay, I promise."

"Yeah?" I muttered. I couldn't get over my feeling of shock. I kept seeing these worst-case scenarios in my head, hearing the wail of the paramedics' siren. . . .

"That's *enough*," Caitlin decided. She climbed to her knees and dug her hands in the snow.

I looked at her with alarm. "What are you doing?"

"What does it look like I'm doing?" she replied, arching her eyebrows. She bunched together a wad of snow and began squeezing it into a ball.

I moved backward. "You don't dare," I said.
"Don't I?"

"No," I said firmly, shaking my finger at her as she gave her snowball an extra squeeze. "Caitlin Dawes, you put that snowball down this instant, or I'll—"

"What?"

"Or I'll think of something."

"That's lame," Caitlin said with a laugh. She hurled the snowball at me. It socked me with a *thwack* right in the center of my chest.

I leaped to my feet. "That's it!" I shouted. "I warned you!" I dove toward her, tackling her to the snow.

We rolled around for a few moments, neither of us getting the upper hand. But finally I managed to flop on top of her.

As I gazed down at her flushed face I realized that she'd never looked more beautiful, more alive, than she did at that moment. So quickly—in just over a month—she had become my entire world.

A second later I was completely lost in the all-encompassing passion of kissing her soft mouth.

Which tasted clean and cold, like freshly fallen snow.

Seven

AFTER I DROPPED Caitlin at home that evening, I drove slowly back to my house. I needed to think. Even though I knew that Caitlin was fine, I still couldn't shake the horrible sensation I'd felt when I'd thought something had happened to her.

Maybe I'm just nervous because everything has been going so well, I thought. After all, I knew that good things couldn't last forever—if things were going well, then soon enough they'd go bad again. I was taking physics in school, and the phrase, *For every action, there is an equal and opposite reaction,* had stuck with me. If that was true, what was the equal reaction to the amazing time I'd been having with Caitlin?

As I pulled into my driveway I forced

myself to stop having those horrible thoughts. Why was I freaking out?

I had to be honest with myself.

I was freaking out because I was falling head over heels in love, something I never thought would happen to me. I was *falling?* I had *fallen.*

And that was a scary place to be.

But it was a place I wasn't about to leave.

I parked in the garage, shut the automatic garage door, and hung my skis on hooks on the wall. When I walked into the house, I shed my ski clothes in the laundry room and stepped into the kitchen.

My mother was waiting for me.

She stood up, scraping back her chair. "Brad, we need to talk."

"Can we do this later?" I asked. "I'm beat."

"Now," she insisted, waving at a chair across from her. "Sit. I have a few things to say."

"Whatever," I said, collapsing into the chair. "What's so important?"

My mother seemed unsure of how to begin. She clasped and unclasped her hands on top of the table.

"Just spit it out, Mom," I prodded.

"It's that girl you're seeing," she said. "Caitlin."

I leaned forward across the table. "What about her?"

My mother put on her worst, sternest expression. "I'm concerned that you're seeing too much of her lately. You're barely ever home. And don't expect me to believe that when the two of you are here while I'm at work that you're doing homework."

I stared back at her without responding. How did she know that Caitlin came over when she wasn't there? I'd certainly never told her.

"Don't you think she's becoming too much of a distraction?" she asked.

I slumped back in my chair. "No," I said. "I don't."

"Well, I think she is," my mother replied. "It's bad enough that you put so much energy into that band of yours—"

"Mom," I interrupted. "Can't you just drop this?"

"No," she said, her voice rising. "It's bad enough you have that band, but now there's Caitlin taking up all the time that you should be studying—"

I stood up. "That's enough. You have no idea what you're talking about."

My mother slammed her hand down on the table, and I jumped, shocked. I hadn't seen her lose her temper in a long time. "Sit *down!*" she yelled. "For once you will listen to me all the way through!"

I sat. "Fine," I muttered, staring down at the table. "So talk."

She took a deep breath. "As I was saying," she continued in a calmer tone of voice, "it seems to me that you're losing sight of what's important. You shouldn't be messing up your schoolwork just because—"

"I'm doing fine in school."

"Please let me finish." My mother swallowed. "You're doing passably, but you could certainly be doing better. You're a very smart boy, and without all these distractions you could be at the top of your class. Easily. Colleges are going to look for dedication and effort. I just think it's time you got serious about your future and cut out all the extras."

"Extras?" I asked. "Caitlin is an extra? My band is an extra? I'm *happy.* That must mean something, even to you. Can't you see I'm happy?"

My mother blinked at me, and for a second I barely recognized her. This person sitting across from me, I had no idea who she was. I wondered wildly if I'd wandered into the wrong house.

"Happiness is fine," she told me, crossing her arms against her chest. "But it shouldn't get in the way of success and accomplishment."

I pressed my hand to my forehead, gaping at

96

her. "Have you been replaced by a *robot?*" I asked. "You can't really believe that."

She sighed. "I don't want to see you mess up your future, Brad."

"Fine," I conceded in a tired voice. "I'll work harder. I'll pay more attention to school. Is that what you want?"

"Yes," she replied. "But I don't think that's enough."

"So then what? What are you telling me?"

My mother gazed directly into my eyes. "That you're too young to be getting so serious about a girl."

"Ohhh-kay," I said slowly, deliberately. "And that means exactly what?"

She raised her chin defiantly. "That you should spend less time with Caitlin and more time on your schoolwork."

"Less time?" I repeated.

"Yes. Once a week should be enough. And you spend way too much time on the phone with her—valuable time that you should be spending on your work."

For a long moment I just stared at her, letting her words sink in, frustration rising inside of me. How dare she tell me how much time to spend with Caitlin! This was the first time I was truly happy in my life, and here she was trying to ruin it for me, giving me all these restrictions.

"You can't be serious," I told her.

"Oh, yes, I am. Once a week with her is plenty of time to—"

"To what?" I interrupted angrily, my fists clenching. "How can you pretend to know how much time I need with Caitlin? She's the most important thing in my life, and you think once a week is just fine?"

"Brad," my mother responded in an annoyingly calm tone, "you're young. Too young to understand—"

"Just stop it!" I burst out, slamming my hands against the edge of the table. "Stop telling me you know better! Caitlin is the best thing that ever happened to me. If you can't see that, then you don't know me at all."

"Brad," my mother began, her voice rising once again. "I'm serious about this. Now stop overreacting and listen to me!"

Overreacting? That put me way over the edge. I jumped to my feet. "I will not ruin my life like you ruined yours!" I screamed at her. "I will not!"

"I'm not asking you to ruin your life," she responded. "I'm trying to save it; I'm trying to help you—"

"By taking away the one thing I love most in the world? Are you *nuts?*"

We glared at each other silently for a moment across the kitchen.

"I'm trying to protect you from getting hurt," my mother said, breaking the tense silence. "I'm just warning you to cool it down before—"

"Before what?" I interrupted. I gripped my hands into fists. "Before *what?*"

"I've learned some harsh lessons—"

"About how to be the coldest person alive!" I finished for her. "I don't have to be like you, you know!"

"No," my mother whispered. "That's not how it is. I've just learned that romantic love doesn't last. You shouldn't give up anything for love, because you can't count on love."

I closed my eyes. The worst part was that in a little corner of my mind, what my mother said made sense. I had watched my father leave, after all. We couldn't count on his love.

No, I ordered myself. *Think of Caitlin.*

Caitlin's face the moment after I kissed her. Her lips a little too red, her cheeks flushed, her eyes swirling with love. I loved her with all my heart. I could never stop loving her.

I opened my eyes and glared at my mother.

"I expect you to do as I ask," she stated. "Or else—"

"Or else what?" I shot back. "You'll kick me out of the house?"

She just blinked back at me, her face turning pale.

"Well, that would be just fine because I don't ever want to talk to you again!" I turned and fled the kitchen, anger surging throughout every cell of my body. As I flew down the stairs toward my bedroom I resolved I would keep my word: I would never talk to my mother again.

Never.

"Would you guys stop smiling at each other like that? It's sickening," Caitlin's sister, Becca, complained as she sat next to us in the Daweses' family room on a Saturday afternoon.

Two months had passed, and things had only gotten worse between my mother and me. There weren't any more fights because I had kept my word and had barely spoken to her. But the frigid silence that filled the house was somehow even worse. My mother and I were strangers living in the same house. I hadn't told Caitlin—or anyone—about our fight.

"We can't help it if we're happy," Caitlin responded, laughing.

That was the truth. I grinned at her, curling a tendril of her hair around my finger. Things were as good as ever between Caitlin and me, which was one of the reasons I hadn't told her about what was going on with my mother.

The last thing I needed was for Caitlin to know that my mother didn't like us hanging out. I wanted our relationship to stay as smooth as possible. And despite my mother's wishes, we still spent plenty of time together. The only difference was that we only hung out at my house when I knew my mother would be working late. We were spending a lot more time at the Daweses' house, much to Becca's dismay—she needed her space. "I'm out of here," she said, rolling her eyes. "If anyone wants me, I'll be upstairs." She jumped up and walked out of the room.

"I hope we're not driving your sister crazy," I said to Caitlin.

"Nah." Caitlin shook her head. "Becca's just used to having things her way. But she's not as annoyed as she pretends to be."

"That's good to know."

At that moment Caitlin's father, a tall man with a gray beard and a little ponytail, peeked his head into the family room. "Hey, kids. What are you up to?"

"Not much. Just hanging out," Caitlin responded.

I smiled to myself, amazed at how different Caitlin's parents were from my mother. If she walked in the room right now, all she would be able to do would be question me about my homework. But Mr. and Mrs. Dawes were laid-back—kind of hippyish, actually. And they were always very welcoming to me.

"How's the band going, Brad?" he asked.

"Great, thanks. I think we're almost ready to perform for an audience soon."

"Don't be so modest," Caitlin said, punching me on the arm playfully. "You guys are incredible!" A couple of weeks before, the band had finally agreed to let Caitlin and Beth come to our rehearsals. They were both unbelievably supportive.

"Well, I can't wait to hear you play," Mr. Dawes told me with a smile, then ducked out of the room.

I glanced down at my watch. "Oooh, I gotta get going," I said. "I'm supposed to be at Ryan's now." Because of the situation with my mother, I had told the guys that we needed to move rehearsals out of my garage. Now we practiced at Ryan's. "You coming?"

"I want to." Caitlin bit her lip, looking torn. "But I really should practice cello today. I have that recital coming up."

I stood up and kissed the top of her head. "Then stay here and practice."

Her big brown eyes opened even wider. "But I want to come hear you. To be there for you."

I laughed. "You've been at every rehearsal for the past couple of weeks—you couldn't be more there for me."

She stood up. "But—"

"No buts," I interrupted. "Tell you what. After practice I'm gonna come over and listen to *you* play."

She smiled brightly. "Sounds good."

"Good." I pulled her into a hug, happiness washing over me.

With Caitlin in my life nothing—not even my mother—could bring me down.

"Hey, guys!" Caitlin sang out as she entered Ryan's garage.

It was about two weeks later, on a sunny Thursday after school, and the guys and I were setting up our instruments for rehearsal. Beth was already there—she'd come over with the rest of us.

Everyone greeted Caitlin, and I walked over to give her a kiss. "Hey, there," I said. "How was your day?"

"All right," she told me. "I think I aced my math test."

"You always do." I squeezed her hand. "Thanks for coming by."

She smiled. "Of course. But I can't stay too long—I've got to practice cello."

"Did you bring it with you?" Ryan called over to us.

We both glanced back at him, confused. "Bring what?" I asked.

He looked at Caitlin. "Your cello."

"It's in my car," she responded.

"Cool," Ryan said, pushing his glasses farther up on his nose. "How about if I record a sample of you playing?"

Caitlin's eyes widened. "My cello?"

"No, the bongos," Ryan teased. "Of course your cello."

"That's a great idea!" I said. I loved listening to Caitlin play. What could be better than getting a recording of it?

Caitlin looked reluctant. "I don't know. . . ."

"Oh, come on," Beth said, putting her hands on her hips. "I've never even heard you play!"

"And it would be cool to have a cello sample for one of our songs," Kenny put in.

"Besides." I nudged her playfully. "You know you're awesome."

Caitlin laughed, her cheeks turning pink. "You're right. I'll be right back." She gave me a peck on the cheek and jogged out of the garage.

"I'm so psyched to hear her!" Beth exclaimed.

"She'll blow you away," I told Beth, feeling proud. I walked over to Ryan, who was setting up the recording equipment. "I'm glad you suggested this," I said to him.

"Yeah." He nodded. "I thought of it the

other day, when you mentioned you were going to her recital."

"Okay, here I am," Caitlin announced. She was standing at the front of the garage, holding her cello next to her. "What now?"

Ryan got her situated, and a couple of minutes later she was sitting in the middle of the garage, poised to play.

Ryan turned a knob and said, "All right, Caitlin—now."

And then she began to play, filling the garage with the graceful sounds of her cello. I recognized the piece right away: Bach Cello Suite Number One—the same song she'd been playing the day I found her in the rehearsal studio at school. This time she had perfected it. And standing there, watching her play in front of all my friends—I was as awestruck as I'd been that very first time I'd heard her.

I couldn't help glancing around at everyone else as they listened. They were all staring at Caitlin, seemingly mesmerized by her talent. When she finished, we burst into applause.

Beth ran over to give her a hug. "That was wonderful!"

Ryan turned off the recording equipment. "Wow, Caitlin, that was really something. Thanks so much."

Caitlin beamed, her eyes lighting up. "No problem."

"That was incredible," Andre told her, running a hand through his hair and looking a bit bewildered. "I mean, really. Incredible."

Kenny slapped me on the back. "Brad-man, that girlfriend of yours knows what she's doing. She rocks!"

She looked up at me, still smiling, and I gave her a wink.

"Believe me," I told Kenny, "I know."

That Saturday, Caitlin and I went sledding on the steep hill behind the elementary school. A new blanket of snow had fallen the night before, and we'd spent the afternoon in competition with dozens of little kids for the best spaces on the hill.

As Caitlin and I walked back toward her house, dragging the plastic sled behind us, her cheeks were red and her lips were blue from the cold. "Do you know how happy you make me?" I asked her.

"Maybe not," she joked, flashing me her teasing smile. "Try me."

"So happy," I said. "Happier than I should be allowed to feel."

And then I felt embarrassed. Because after all the time we'd spent together, after how close we'd become, after how important she'd become to me, I'd never actually said the words. I'd never told her I loved her.

I linked my arm through hers, and we continued toward her house.

I *wanted* to tell her. I'd even come close a few times. Once while we were quietly doing our homework and I looked at her—she was deep in concentration, and I was just burning with the need to tell her I loved her. But that time she'd glanced up and asked me a question about geology, and the moment passed on by.

Soon. *I will tell her soon*, I promised myself. Because she deserved to hear it, and because it was true.

As we trudged up her lawn together I asked myself, *So, then, what's the problem? Why can't you say the words you need to say?*

Because those three little words sounded too much like a promise. It was one thing to write a song like "Continental Divide," but it was a complete other thing to say the words out loud right to her face. As much as I wanted to believe I could keep my promise forever, my mother's warnings still echoed in my mind.

I learned that romantic love doesn't last. . . .

I bit my lip as I followed Caitlin into the house, leaving the sled out on the stoop. Soon. I would prove my mother wrong and make my promise to Caitlin. Soon.

Caitlin's parents had a fire crackling in the living-room fireplace, but they were both in the kitchen, fixing dinner. I said hello and made my way into the living room, where I collapsed onto the couch, close enough to feel the flickering warmth of the fire. Caitlin joined me a few minutes later, bringing two mugs of steaming hot cocoa.

We cuddled together on the couch, not saying much, just sipping our cocoa and warming up in front of the fire. Caitlin rested her head on my chest, and I stroked her long, impossibly soft hair.

It hit me. This was love. Warmth and security, a trusting body to rest against, a comfortable silence. I could have spoken if I'd wanted to—Caitlin would have listened and made an intelligent, thoughtful response. I could ask her to get up and tango, and she would have played along. But we didn't need to do those things because, at the very bottom of it all, we just had to *be* together. And amazingly, wonderfully, that was plenty.

"I love you," I whispered into her ear. And I had to blink away a sudden tear because it had been so easy to say.

Caitlin snuggled up closer against me. "I love you too," she said.

And that was it. The most perfect moment of my life.

Eight

Spring in Colorado was an amazing event.

After the months of gray winter weather the skies brightened, the trees turned green again, and best of all, the whole town *rioted* with flowers. Boulder is nuts about flowers. The long outdoor aisles of the Sixteenth Street Mall erupted in red tulips, and it seemed like every street had a display of incredible blossoms.

Caitlin and I took advantage of a warm, sunny Saturday and had a picnic in our neighborhood park. We spread out an old blanket under a crab apple tree covered with bright pink petals and listened to music on my portable CD player as we ate tuna sandwiches and drank sun tea.

I spent most of the time lying on my back with my face in the sun, occasionally stealing glimpses of Caitlin out of the corner of my eye. She sat cross-legged, engrossed in a Margaret Atwood novel.

Then I noticed her hand tremble as she absently turned a page.

I sat up. "What was that?" I asked.

Caitlin glanced up at me. "What? Did you hear something?"

"Your hand," I said. "You were shaking. Are you cold?"

"Well, it *is* breezy . . . but no, I'm warm enough," she replied. Caitlin put the book facedown in her lap and held up her hands. They seemed rock steady.

"I guess it was nothing," I said.

She shrugged and picked up her book again. "I've been stretching the muscles in my hand a little," she told me. "I'm trying to extend my reach in my fingerings. They're probably spasming in protest."

Caitlin's hands got cramped sometimes from playing the cello too much. All the fingers on her right hand had these thick calluses on the tips from pressing against the strings. I shifted over and took her right hand in mine. She returned to her book as I played with her fingers. The calluses felt cool—I knew they had a kind of power in them because they helped her play her beautiful music.

"Will you read to me?" I murmured.

"I'm already in the middle. It won't make any sense to you."

I rearranged my body on the blanket and rested my head in her lap. "I don't care," I said. "Just read to me. I want to hear your voice."

"Okay," she agreed.

As Caitlin read I drifted, listening, surrounded by warm spring air, the sweet scent of the blossoming tree above us, the chirp of a bird in the tree, and the wonderful feel of Caitlin herself. In that perfect way we spent the rest of the afternoon.

"I'll stop over at your place and get that Billie Holiday CD," Caitlin said as we were packing up to go home. She stuffed the sun tea bottle into her backpack. "Okay?"

"Uh . . . ," I began, stalling for time. There was a good chance my mother was home. But she'd been home a lot lately over the past month, and I was running out of excuses to keep Caitlin away. "The place is a mess," I fibbed. "I'll just run in and get it, and we'll go over to your house."

She didn't look at me as she zipped up her bag. "Can I ask you a question?"

"Sure."

"Is there some reason you don't want me in your house?"

"Why would you say that?" I asked, staring at the ground.

Now Caitlin faced me full on, her eyebrows raised. "Oh, maybe because I haven't been over there in, like, three weeks? Sheer coincidence? And why do you always make up such lame excuses whenever I suggest we go there?"

As if I could lie to her when her big brown eyes were focused on me so intensely. "Uh," I said, "it's just—"

"It's just what?"

"Nothing," I finished. I was trapped, and I knew it. I only hoped my mother had left the house. "What's a little clutter?" I joked feebly. "Of course you can come in. Don't be silly."

Ten minutes later we were at my front door. My mother's car wasn't in the driveway, but that meant nothing. She could have parked in the garage. Heart hammering, I led Caitlin inside.

Mom stood beside the microwave in the kitchen. She glanced at us in surprise as we walked in.

"Uh, hi, Mom," I said quickly. "Caitlin and I are just here to pick up . . . something." That was the most I'd said to her—besides things like "We need more milk" or "The dishwasher's busted"—since our fight.

My mother just nodded. She pulled a steaming mug from the microwave and dropped a tea bag in it.

"Hi, Ms. Sullivan," Caitlin called out.

"Hello," my mother said shortly, then stalked off toward her bedroom. She left the microwave door open and her mug of tea just sitting on the counter.

I closed my eyes and sighed. How was I supposed to explain her rude behavior to Caitlin?

"What was that about?" she asked. "Did I do something wrong?"

I opened my eyes to look at her seriously. "No," I assured her. "It's not you. My mother and I are having sort of a fight."

"A big one? What about?"

"Yeah," I admitted, "it's pretty big. We kind of aren't speaking to each other."

"What's the fight about?" Caitlin asked again.

I'd heard her the first time. To avoid answering, I walked over and closed the microwave door. "Uh," I replied. "She got pushy about school, and we ended up screaming at each other."

"How long has this been going on?"

I opened up the refrigerator and peered inside. Nothing looked all that appealing. "A while," I answered.

"How long is a while?"

I turned to face her. "A few months," I said quickly. "C'mon, let's go get the Billie Holiday CD. I've got the whole collection—"

"A few *months?*" Caitlin was shocked. "You haven't spoken to each other in *months?*"

"Yeah," I replied. "It was a nasty fight. We both said . . . some things." I took her hands in mine. "Really," I said. "It's not a big deal. Don't go making a big deal out of this."

Caitlin slipped her hands out of mine. "It sounds like a big deal to me. Is that why you didn't want me to come over here?"

I shrugged. "Can't we just drop it?"

"How can you live like this?" Caitlin persisted. "Isn't it awful in here all the time? The silence?"

I shook my head slowly. "There have been some rough spots," I said, "but it'll be okay. I've gotten used to it—"

"She was probably just reaching out to you," Caitlin interrupted, her eyes a little glazed over as she thought about it. "Like I said, her being all strict about your school-work is probably just her way of showing concern."

I couldn't help giving a little laugh. "I definitely doubt that."

"No, really," Caitlin continued. "Her

methods are clumsy and all *wrong,* but she's just trying to communicate, I have a feeling."

"Keep your voice down," I told Caitlin, glancing nervously toward my mother's room. "I think the communication thing is more about *your* mother and *you.* I have a whole different set of problems."

"Don't you miss her? At all?"

I sat down in one of the kitchen chairs. "Yeah, okay," I said. "Sometimes it would be nice if this war was over, but it's all right."

"She's not the most open person, is she?" Caitlin asked.

I laughed. "That's the world's biggest understatement."

Caitlin sat down next to me. "Well, then, it's up to you to reach out to her," she told me solemnly. "*You* have to close the distance between you two."

I wanted to laugh again, but Caitlin seemed so concerned that I knew she wouldn't understand why I was laughing. "You don't get it," I said softly. "And that's fine. This is between my mother and me."

"I just think you need to forgive her and move on."

That was my Caitlin—warm and forgiving, always believing the best in people. And I couldn't fault her for being so off base. After all, she had no idea that *she* was the real

115

reason my mother and I weren't speaking.

But I wasn't so forgiving. Not when some-one—*anyone*—tried to get between me and the girl I loved.

I reached out to Caitlin and pulled her onto my lap. "You have the biggest heart of anyone I've ever met," I whispered into her hair, wrapping my arms around her.

"I think you'd be surprised at the size of your own if you give it a chance."

That time I did laugh. "Whatever," I said. "*Now* can we go over to your place? I want to hear what Billie sounds like in your room any-way. I'll bet it's a completely different experi-ence."

"Sure," Caitlin replied.

"Okay, *up,*" I said, slapping the sides of my thighs. Caitlin hopped off me. "I'll be right back," I told her. "I'll just run down and get the CD."

It took me a few minutes to locate the disc in my collection. I promised myself for the thousandth time that I'd eventually get around to organizing the whole mess alphabetically. But that would be a major project. Finally I found it, and I headed back upstairs.

Caitlin wasn't in the kitchen.

After a moment of confusion, I heard voices coming from down the hall—from my mother's bedroom. Quietly I stepped closer. Was Caitlin talking to my *mother?*

She sure was. A terrible gnawing feeling started in my stomach as I edged down the hall to hear better.

"Oh, practicing my cello mostly," I heard Caitlin say.

Then my mother said something I couldn't make out.

"Oh, yes," Caitlin replied politely. "I study cello in school. . . . Brad never told you?"

Again I couldn't hear my mother's answer.

"And I hang out with Brad a lot, of course," Caitlin continued. She didn't sound nervous at all, which was weird since my mother inspired that reaction in almost everyone.

There was silence for a moment in the bedroom. "You should know," Caitlin suddenly blurted, "Brad regrets the fight you had. He'd like for you two to be talking again."

My stomach twisted in a knot so painful, it was almost a cramp. *What* did she say? *How dare she!* I thought, anger steaming up within me. I ran the rest of the way down the hall and burst into my mother's bedroom.

My mother was sitting on her bed with a newspaper spread across her lap. Caitlin was standing at the foot of the bed. They both turned to look at me.

"What are you *saying* to her?" I yelled at Caitlin. "Get out of here!"

117

Caitlin blinked at me, surprised. "We were just talking—"

"That's *enough* talking!" I shouted. I couldn't believe Caitlin had done this to me, talking about me behind my back—with my mother, of all people. I grabbed her arm, pulling her toward the door. "Get out of here, now."

Caitlin pulled her arm away. "Brad, wait—"

"Now!" I screamed.

But she didn't move. I stared at her, my heart racing, my hands shaking. I refused to even look at my mother.

"Listen," Caitlin said, holding up her hands, "if we all just talk about this—"

"It's none of your business!" I hollered. "It's none of your business *at all!*"

I had never yelled at her before. Caitlin flinched, and my heart squeezed in pain. But somehow that just made me feel more furious.

After a second of frozen silence in the room, I spun around and ran out.

Caitlin caught up to me in the kitchen. "Brad, wait," she called again.

"You have no idea what you were just doing in there," I told her through clenched teeth. "No idea at all."

"I was just trying to make things right—"

"Well, don't," I spat out. I glared at her, only becoming more angry by the hurt look in her eyes. How dare *she* feel hurt? How could someone I loved so deeply betray me so completely? My whole body was shaking. "I can't trust you anymore," I told her. "Really. I can never trust you again."

Tears filled her eyes, and she clumsily wiped them away with the back of her hand. "Brad," she whimpered.

I turned away from her and walked over to the sink, staring down into the drain. At that moment I wanted nothing more than to be as far away from her as possible.

"Brad," Caitlin sobbed. "I was just—"

"No!" I shouted, banging my hands on the sides of the sink. "Just stop, okay? Just *shut up!*"

She made a noise then—a choked, wet sound that twisted something inside me, some organ I hadn't even known I had. I opened my mouth in a soundless moan.

"Okay," she whispered. "Okay."

I stood there, staring down the drain, until I heard Caitlin walk out of the kitchen. And when I heard her open and close the front door as she left the house, I knew my days of happiness were over.

Nine

I WASN'T SURE how long I remained in the same position over the sink. All I knew was that I was simmering with anger.

How could she do this to me? I thought.

Then I turned the water on in the sink, for no real reason except that the faucet was right there in front of me. I watched the water swirl around, picking up some random suds, and spiral into the drain.

I'll be better off without her, I thought as I heard the television start blaring loudly from my mother's room. *I could spend more time with my band, I could concentrate more on school. . . .*

I stuck my finger into the swirling water in the sink.

That was my whole life, going down the drain.

Stupid tears started to trickle down my cheeks. It was all over. Caitlin and I were through.

Miserable, I stuck my hands into the cold water and splashed some on my face. That helped nothing—now I was just miserable and wet.

Slouching over onto the countertop, I buried my face in my arms.

Was I out of my mind? What had she done that was so terrible? Caitlin had only wanted me to make up with my mother, that's all. Sure, she'd gone behind my back to do it, but she'd thought that my mother and I were only fighting about school—some stupid, minor argument. She hadn't known how serious the fight was. How could she have known? I hadn't told her.

Caitlin was only trying to do what she did best—make peace, figure out people's problems, make them feel better. She'd only been trying to help.

She'd only been trying to help me. And I'd freaked out all over her.

I stood up straight, sniffled away my tears, and swallowed them down. There was no way I was going to lose her.

I ran out the front door, heading over to her place. Caitlin would forgive me—she had to because I couldn't survive without her. I'd

712010 116__ L-M6 07/29/98

POLYNESIAN
CULTURAL CENTER

All the spirit of the islands. All in one place.

Purchase our video trio special
for only $43 & receive a FREE
Horizons compact disc. Save $37

712010 1167 L-MO 07/29/98

FREE 35 minute Laie Tour to the
Hawaii Temple and BYUH Campus.
Every 20 min. from 1:40-7:00 pm

DISCLAIMER:

By using this ticket to enter the Polynesian Cultural Center (PCC) the user acknowledges that he knows the risks and dangers may arise during the use of the premises and that the user assumes all risks of injury to person or property that may be sustained in connection with the use of the premises. In consideration for the permission to enter the premises, user of this ticket hereby releases and discharges PCC and its employees from any and/or claim of any sort of injury to person and/or property due to the negligence or any other cause during the use of the premises. This ticket is not subject to refund (including inclement weather).

4525131

INVALID IF STUB IS REMOVED

INVALID IF STUB IS REMOVED

POLYNESIAN
CULTURAL CENTER

All the spirit of the islands. All in one place.

712010 1167 G-JRS 07/23/98

CHILD

GUIDE

JUNIOR

07/29/98

DISCLAIMER:

By using this ticket to enter the Polynesian Cultural Center (PCC) the user acknowledges that he knows the risks and dangers may arise during the use of the premises and that the user assumes all risks of injury to person or property that may be sustained in connection with the use of the premises. In consideration for the permission to enter the premises, user of this ticket hereby releases and discharges PCC and its employees from any and/or claim of any sort of injury to person and/or property due to the negligence or any other cause during the use of the premises. This ticket is not subject to refund (including inclement weather).

5-5-R-63

Port Sec Row   Seat

08/03/98

Evening Show

8:00 pm

Pacific Theater
Horizons! Where the Sea
meets the Sky

ADULT

712015 935 B-D25 08/03/98

POLYNESIAN
CULTURAL CENTER

All the spirit of the islands. All in one place.

Purchase our video trio special
for only $43 & receive a FREE
Horizons compact disc. Save $37.

712015 935 B-D25 SB 08/03/98

DISCLAIMER:

By using this ticket to enter the Polynesian Cultural Center (PCC) the user acknowledges that he knows the risks and dangers may arise during the use of the premises and that the user assumes all risks of injury to person or property that may be sustained in connection with the use of the premises. In consideration for the permission to enter the premises, user of this ticket hereby releases and discharges PCC and its employees from any and/or claim of any sort of injury to person and/or property due to the negligence or any other cause during the use of the premises. This ticket is not subject to refund (including inclement weather).

4513166

INVALID IF STUB
IS REMOVED

explain that I'd been stupid, and why I'd lost my temper. . . .

When I got to her house, I rang the bell, panting heavily. I thought about what I would say when she opened the door. Should I just drop to my knees and beg? I'd do that. Or maybe I should just show her how sad I was, let her read my misery from my face, tell her I loved her. . . .

Becca opened the door. "What do *you* want?" she asked rudely.

"Becca!" I said. "Can I speak to Caitlin? Is she here? Can I speak to her, please?"

Becca leaned against the door frame. "What did you do to her anyway?"

"We had a fight," I explained. "C'mon, will you just tell her I'm here?"

With a shrug Becca stepped back. "She's not here. She took her car."

"Did she say where she was going?"

"She didn't say anything to me," Becca replied. "All I know is that she was a total mess—tears, the works. If you've hurt her, you're going to hear from me. I hope you know that."

"Fine," I said as Becca closed the door.

I didn't know where to start searching. Caitlin had taken her car, which meant she could be anywhere. I jogged back home to get my Jetta.

At first I just drove around Boulder, hoping to catch sight of her green Honda. I didn't have a destination in mind—I just followed the road, turning when there was a light. I wandered aimlessly, keeping my eyes peeled for any sign of her.

Then, outside the King Soopers supermarket parking lot, I spotted a green Honda. My heart leaped. I veered over to the Honda with a screech, cutting across a lane of traffic.

I ignored the blares of the car horns and pulled up alongside the Honda. Waving frantically, I tried to get Caitlin's attention.

Except it wasn't Caitlin. This tiny old woman was driving the green Honda. And she looked absolutely terrified of me.

Sorry, I mouthed at her, feeling my cheeks burn with embarrassment.

I let her drive on ahead of me as I shook my head, wondering what was wrong with me. *Brad, get a grip,* I scolded myself. Just because I wanted to find Caitlin was no reason to lose my mind entirely.

And anyway, I was taking absolutely the wrong approach. I knew my girlfriend. She wouldn't just drive around—she'd *go* someplace. Someplace she'd feel safe, to think things over.

I headed toward the September School. She was probably in one of the music rooms, working out all the horrible things I'd said to her on her cello.

Less than ten minutes later I was racing down the hallway toward that big sunset painting, peeking into all the windows of the music rooms. But the September School was entirely deserted. I even cracked open the door to the girls' bathroom and called out Caitlin's name. No answer. She wasn't there. I double-checked the music rooms again, just to be sure, but finally I had to accept that I was on the wrong track.

My heart sank as I hurried back to my car. Where else could she have gone?

Over the next couple of hours I drove from place to place, coming up empty. I stopped by Café Roma, Penny Lane, a coffee shop called Buchanan's, and another café-bookstore named Trident. As I then drove from park to park my stomach started to churn. It was starting to get dark, and I still hadn't found her. Where could she have gone? Then I started to get scared. What if something had happened to her, something bad?

I drove around, searching the streets until my eyes hurt. Darkness settled in, and each lonely street lamp that I passed reminded me of that first kiss we'd shared in the snowy mountains. I gripped the steering wheel until my knuckles turned white.

Soon it was too dark to see anymore. She could be in any shadow. I gave up and headed home.

I would call her the moment I stepped into my house. *Caitlin,* I said to her silently, *please, please forgive me. I'm so sorry. You are everything to me.*

Miserably I pulled the Jetta into my driveway and parked. I sat in the car for a moment, just feeling overwhelmed with worry. Then I climbed out of the car and trudged toward the house.

As I came around the corner I saw Caitlin sitting on the front step. She'd been hidden from view by the hedges. I stopped short, paralyzed with relief.

Caitlin smiled—that radiant smile—and I ran to her. I swept her into my arms, pressing my mouth against her neck, breathing in her wonderful scent, her hair tickling my cheek.

"I'm so sorry," she whispered.

I stepped back and held her at arm's length so I could look into her face. "No," I said. "Not you. It's all my fault. You shouldn't apologize for anything."

"But I shouldn't have—"

"No," I repeated. "This is all my apology. I'm more sorry than I've been about anything in my life. I've been driving around searching

126

for you this whole time. I do trust you, Caitlin. Will you forgive me?"

She ducked her head, a faint blush coloring her cheeks. "It wasn't any of my business," she said. "I was just trying to—"

"Help," I finished for her. "I know, I know that. It took me a while, but I figured that out. Just say you'll forgive me."

Caitlin glanced up, her eyes searing me with their intensity. "How could I do anything else?" she whispered.

I kissed her, and happiness flowed through my body so powerfully that my knees felt weak. We sat down together on the step. I didn't want to let go of her for a single second.

"I won't meddle anymore," Caitlin said. "The things between you and your mother are none of my business. I promise, I won't poke my nose in where it doesn't belong."

I kissed the tip of her nose. "You poke your nose wherever you like," I murmured. "Your business is whatever you care about, okay?"

"Okay."

I slipped my hand around her soft neck, feeling her pulse under my hand, and pulled her close until our foreheads were pressed together gently. "But just this once, can I deal with my mother in my own way? That's all I ask, just to handle it my own way."

"I promise," Caitlin said solemnly.

"Thank you," I replied, and I enveloped her in a big hug. And I felt finally, absolutely complete.

All during my search for Caitlin, I'd been out of my mind with fear—fear that something stupid could come between us, fear that we could ever be separated, fear that anything could make our love die.

But now I knew that would never happen. Because the love I felt for her could rise above anything, I was sure of it.

I kissed her warm lips, promising myself I would never allow us to drift apart, never. I would never lose her, no matter what. I couldn't.

No matter what.

Ten

THE THUNDEROUS WAVE of applause was one of the best sounds I'd ever heard in my life.

I hopped off the stage at Penny Lane with a big grin, waving at the audience. They were still cheering, but it was slacking off. I never wanted the applause to end. Once you heard that sound—those cheers—you craved it like a drug.

As the deejay started up a song I turned to my band mates, who were following me offstage. They all had goofy smiles on their faces. At that moment I realized that these guys—all of them, Jeff, Ryan, Andre, and Kenny—were the best friends anyone could ever ask for. And Tomorrowland had just blown the crowd away.

"I wish we could play, like, forever," Jeff told us, his eyes flashing with excitement. "That rocked so hard!"

"Whoo!" Kenny yelled, waving his hands in the air. "I am just so pumped *up!*" He shook his sweaty, long blond hair. "Did you see their faces? Do you *know* how many girls were smiling at me?"

"Many," Andre replied.

Kenny grabbed Andre's arms and shook him. Andre didn't even blink. "You saw it too, didn't you? I wasn't dreaming!" Kenny insisted. He turned to me and Ryan. "I've got proof! Andre saw it too!"

Andre nodded slowly. "I felt the vibe."

I laughed and shoved Kenny playfully. "Well, go get 'em, stud-boy."

Kenny laughed too. He slipped behind Andre and Jeff and started pushing them into the crowd. "Let's go! We are gonna be some happy men tonight!"

Ryan and I looked at each other and cracked up. "Boy's out of control." Ryan shook his head.

"Testosterone's fried his poor little brain," I agreed. "But can you blame him for being psyched?"

"Not me!" Ryan replied with a smile. "I'm about to get my reward now." He nodded toward the milling throng of people, where Beth and Caitlin were pushing toward us.

Beth made it to us first and hugged Ryan. "You guys were *awesome,*" she cried, her blond ponytail swinging. "I told you it would go off like clockwork. You rehearsed so much, how could it not?"

Beth turned to me and squeezed my arm. "Brad, you were great up there—your voice gets better every time I hear it."

"Thanks," I replied.

But then Beth glanced at Caitlin, who was dawdling toward us, and her clear blue eyes flickered with concern. "You'd better check on her," Beth told me. "I don't think she's doing so hot—"

The next second I was by Caitlin's side. "What's the matter?" I asked. "Beth said—"

"It's nothing," Caitlin interrupted, giving me a small smile. "I just got a headache from the music, that's all."

I looked closely into her face. Her eyes were narrow, her mouth was pressed together tightly enough to turn it grayish white, and her forehead was furrowed with tension. "You're in pain," I said. "We weren't *that* bad, were we?"

She slid her arms around me and rested her head against my chest. "You were wonderful," she murmured. "That's the best I've seen yet. You just keep getting better and better.

'Continental Divide' is my favorite—that song's just so beautiful."

I chuckled. "You just like it because it's about you," I teased.

She squeezed me. "Of course."

I gently tilted up her chin with my finger. "Are you sure you're all right?" I asked.

She nodded. "I'm okay. I just need an aspirin or something. I'll be fine."

There was a tap on my shoulder. I turned to see Duane, the booker in charge of setting up Penny Lane's schedule. He was a longtime fixture on the Boulder music scene—everybody knew Duane. I let go of Caitlin and shook Duane's offered hand, my stomach twisting a little in excitement.

Duane was an older, shortish guy with a shiny bald head and a long fringe of hair in back. He had a massive potbelly under a too tight white oxford shirt. "Good show," Duane said, his face betraying no emotion.

"Oh . . . thanks," I replied nervously. Duane had the power to crush my good mood—or send it into the stratosphere.

"Yeah," Duane continued. "Major improvement from last time."

"Thanks," I said again. Then I just blurted, "So, we get a gig here or what?"

Duane stroked his chin where he was growing in a patchy goatee. "I'll be honest with you,

Myers," he answered, "because I like you. I think you're a good kid. Tomorrowland's not really right for Penny Lane."

My stomach sank. "But the crowd loved us," I protested.

He shook his head. "I'm just telling you my gut feeling. You aren't right for Penny Lane. The dance music night's not getting a lot of attention, and the crowds just aren't coming in. Too many of the college kids want sixties-, seventies-sounding rock, you know what I mean? But—"

"So I guess that's that," I interrupted.

Duane snorted. "I wasn't done," he said. "Listen up. I'm producing a rave two weeks from Saturday up in the mountains. Big crowd, and Tomorrowland's their kind of band. I'll give you a half hour in the middle if you want in."

A rave! That was way better than Penny Lane's tiny music night.

"Oh, wow, yes," I told Duane. "We're there."

"Cool," Duane said with a nod. He dug into his back pocket and pulled out a brightly colored invite. "You'll probably go on something like two A.M.—which is prime time, if you ask me. But you should be there from the start 'cause the schedule's notorious for being shuffled around."

"Excellent," I said. I stuck out my hand, and Duane shook it. "Thanks, Duane," I told him. "You're the best."

"No biggie," Duane said. "You guys impressed me tonight. Keep it up."

I couldn't help smiling like an idiot as he turned away and disappeared into the crowd. A rave! The guys would be so psyched. We could even start getting noticed in the whole dance music scene.

Caitlin put her hand on my shoulder. "Any second now you're going to be the *famous* Brad Myers," she said. "Let's see that invite."

We looked at it together. In swirling, psychedelic colors the card showed a guy and a girl intertwined like the trunk of a tree, their arms stretching out to become the branches. On top it read, *Welcome to Eden.*

"Looks cool," Caitlin murmured in a shaky voice.

I turned to face her, surging with worry. She sounded terrible, her voice little more than a croak. She was extremely pale and wobbly on her feet.

"Caitlin," I said in alarm. "What's wrong?"

She waved her hand at me. "Just the headache," she replied. "I think I need to sit down."

I led her carefully over to a chair and eased her into it. "You don't look good at all," I told her. "I mean, you look beautiful, but—"

"I'm fine," Caitlin broke in sharply. "It's just a headache from the music. It *was* loud, you know."

I leaned down and kissed her forehead. "Okay," I replied. "You know best."

"And don't you forget it."

She leaned against me. If Caitlin told me not to worry, I wouldn't worry. But she looked so pale. . . . I gently stroked her hair.

Right then a whole crowd of kids my age wandered over, telling me how much they liked our show, complimenting my singing, wanting to shake my hand.

And I turned away from Caitlin toward their wonderful words of praise.

I spent the next week frantically trying to pull a great set together for the rave with the band. It had to be perfect because this was our first real chance at getting our name out there, at becoming known. If Tomorrowland was going to make it—and we *were* going to make it—our first real gig had to change the ravers' worlds. We swore a Tomorrowland pact that everyone at the rave would dance until they dropped . . . or we'd die trying.

When I wasn't whipping the guys into shape, I was worrying about Caitlin. Her headaches hadn't gone away. Twice when I called her in the early evening, her mother told me that she'd already gone to sleep, trying to escape the pain. Between the band and her headaches, I didn't get to see much of her.

Finally on Monday afternoon she went to the doctor. I sat at home in a panic the whole time she was gone, waiting to hear what was wrong. A dark, back corner of my mind kept pushing forward these horrifying scenarios, and I kept pushing them away again. It's not like anything could be seriously wrong. I sat on my bed and tried to do my science homework, which was spread out beside me. But I also had the phone on my bed—and every ten minutes or so I'd call the Daweses' house, checking to see if she'd come home yet. Becca was getting frustrated with me.

Finally on my fifth call Becca lost patience. "Brad," she told me in her no-nonsense voice, "don't you *dare* call here again. If I pick up this phone and hear your voice one more time, I'll . . . I'll never take a message from you again."

"That's so unfair," I protested.

"Tough," Becca replied. "You're so nervous, you're starting to freak *me* out. And neither of us should be freaking. Because Caitlin's fine."

"I know, I know." I sighed. "Just tell her I called, okay?"

"Like I wouldn't," Becca said. "Duh." She hung up.

Finally an hour later Caitlin called. "Hey, it's me," she said when I answered. She sounded tired.

I sat up on the edge of my bed. "What'd the doctor say?"

She groaned. "That was a complete waste of time," she told me. "He did a few tests and mostly asked me all these questions."

"So that's good?" I asked quickly. "I mean, if he didn't find anything wrong, that's good, right?"

"Brad," Caitlin said, her voice heavy, "don't give me a hard time. My parents have been so annoying about this whole thing." She sounded more than tired, actually—she was downright cranky.

"Sorry," I mumbled. "So what kind of questions did he ask?"

"All this stuff," she replied. "How I'm adjusting to school, when the headaches started, how bad they get, where the pain is, everything you can think of. He wanted to know what kind of stress I'm under, what my hormonal cycles have been like, how I adjusted to the move here, how I've been feeling otherwise. . . . It was exhausting."

"Did you come up with any reasons? Stressful stuff? That could be why, right?"

137

"I guess so," she answered. "I have been under a lot of pressure at school, just keeping up. They push us hard there."

"Uh-huh." The September School seemed funky and carefree from the outside, but Caitlin's music teachers were extremely demanding. I supposed that they saw her talent and wanted to make sure she reached her full potential. But it meant that Caitlin had to practice her cello for several hours a day, and she always worried about being a disappointment.

"Can you take it easier?" I asked. "I mean, I know you have to work hard, but can you ease off a bit?"

"I don't know if that's a good idea," she said slowly. "There's this girl, Clara, who wants my spot in the orchestra—"

"You didn't tell me about her."

"I'm telling you now," she shot back, still sounding snippy. I let it slide. "Clara's really good," Caitlin continued, "and I don't know if I should relax around her with the way things are going. I *love* being in the orchestra, and I don't want to lose my seat—"

"You won't," I promised quickly. "You're the best."

"It takes work to be the best," Caitlin replied. "This girl Clara has like no life—all she does is practice. And so many other things take up my time. . . ."

With a pang, I got the hint. *I* was taking up her time. "We don't have to see so much of each other," I said, unable to keep a note of hurt from creeping into my voice. "If it would help you, we can see each other only on weekends . . . or less. . . ."

Caitlin didn't reply for a long moment. Of course, I was hoping that she wanted to see me—needed to see me—as much as I longed to be with her. But if it would help her headaches go away, I'd see her only once a month. And it wasn't like I didn't have my own things to keep me busy. I had the band—

"No," Caitlin answered. "That's not what I want at all, Brad. You know that."

I felt a selfish bolt of pleasure that I was as important to her as her music. After all, I wouldn't rate Tomorrowland over her! "Good," I said. "Good."

"Besides," she told me, "even musically, not seeing you would be a mistake. The more living you do, the better you are, the more passion and wisdom you can put into the music." She dropped her voice to a whisper. "And you make me feel more alive than anything."

I swallowed. Everything she'd said was so true for me as well. "I love you," I said.

"I love you too."

"So," I began again, shaking my head to

clear it. "What did the doctor finally decide? What comes next?"

"Well, Dr. Loggia said that next comes a lot of tests, the X rays and CAT scans and the blood work. All that stuff gives me the creeps." I heard a tremor in her voice. "He gave me a prescription for some serious headache medicine," she continued, "and told me if the headaches didn't go away after ten days that I should come back in and we'd start the whole testing procedure."

"Good." I sighed with relief. "So it seems like you're okay. Overall."

"Overall," she agreed. "I'll try relaxing more and eat those pills. And we'll see how it goes."

I felt a burst of confidence. Of course Caitlin would be okay. How could she not be? "Great," I said with finality. "Okay, back to this Clara person. I just know you'll knock her back where she belongs. I don't care what you say—you *are* the best."

"I know," Caitlin said. And she laughed.

Two days later I finally got to see her again. I'd written new lyrics for a song we were planning to start off with at the rave, and I couldn't wait to show them to her. The song was called "Sway"—it wasn't as personal as some of the other stuff I'd been working on, but it was fun.

I went over to her place on Wednesday evening, when I knew she'd be finishing up dinner with her family.

Caitlin's mother let me in. "Hi, Brad," she said with a big smile that was just as pretty as Caitlin's. "C'mon in. Doug and I are just having tea in the kitchen."

Doug was Mr. Dawes. Caitlin's parents always tried to get me to call them Caroline and Doug, but I just couldn't. It was too ingrained in me to call parents Mr. and Mrs.—or at least Mr. and Ms.

I followed Mrs. Dawes into the kitchen. "Hey, rock star boy!" Mr. Dawes boomed out from his seat behind the big oak table when he saw me.

I grinned. "I *told* you, Mr. Dawes," I replied. "I don't play rock music."

He waved his hands at me dismissively. "Pop, techno, new wave, electronica, whatever," he responded. "It's all rock and roll to me."

"Have a seat, Brad," Mrs. Dawes told me. "Would you like some herbal tea? We've got peppermint. It's very soothing."

"Uh, no thanks," I answered. "Is Caitlin around?" I didn't mean to be rude, but all parents—no matter how cool they were—made me feel a little nervous.

"She took a nap before dinner," Mrs. Dawes replied. "The migraines again. She told me to wake her when you got here, but let's give her a few minutes more, okay?"

I sat down at the table directly across from Mr. Dawes. "The doctor called her headaches migraines?" I asked.

Mrs. Dawes sat down beside me and slipped her hand into the handle of her oversized mug of tea. "Not really," she said. "But I got migraines when I was her age—just growing pains, my mother used to say—and that's what I bet they are."

"That's good to know," I told her.

Mr. Dawes leaned across the table. "So," he said in his slightly too loud voice, "my daughter tells me you got a gig this weekend."

I smiled. Most parents would sound stupid saying a word like *gig,* but Mr. Dawes managed it okay. I could tell he'd been to his share of concerts—probably The Grateful Dead or The Rolling Stones—but that was close enough. *My* mother hadn't been to a concert in her entire life except the symphony. "That's right," I replied. "At a rave up in the mountains. I can't even tell you how excited I am."

"I heard it starts pretty late," Mrs. Dawes said. She took a sip of her tea. "Actually, *very* late."

"Yeah," I admitted. "We're not even scheduled to go on until two."

Mr. Dawes rubbed his chin. "You know, of course, we don't usually allow Caitlin to be out that late," he told me. "But we've made an exception. I heard her friend Beth will be there too."

"Yes," I said quickly. I hadn't even considered the fact that Caitlin might not be allowed to go. The thought of performing without her in the crowd made my stomach drop. "Beth will be there, and it's a well-organized event, or at least it's supposed to be. There's always police and an ambulance nearby—"

"It's not that I don't trust you," Mr. Dawes began. Then he stopped and smiled. "Oh, of course I don't trust you. There's not a young man alive I'd trust with my daughter at two in the morning. But I trust Caitlin."

"You should," I put in hastily. "She's very trustworthy."

Mr. Dawes laughed, and Mrs. Dawes smiled. "We know how important her being there is to you," Mrs. Dawes said. "So we gave her permission."

"Yeah," Mr. Dawes agreed. "But I'll tell you one thing—you're lucky we didn't decide to come along as chaperons."

I smiled. "You'd be welcome. And if you and Mrs. Dawes showed up at the rave, I think I could safely say that you'd be the hippest parents in Boulder."

"I'd hate to pass that title up." Mrs. Dawes shook her head. "But two A.M. is a little late—even for us."

"Although we still really want to come hear you play," Mr. Dawes added.

"Well, hopefully we'll be playing again soon . . . at an earlier show."

"We'll be there," Mrs. Dawes promised.

Suddenly I heard music sifting into the kitchen from upstairs. Cello. Even muffled by the walls and the ceiling, it sounded wonderful. I cocked my head. "I think someone's awake," I said.

Mrs. Dawes nodded. "Go on up," she told me. "And ask her if she's hungry. I saved a plate for her from dinner."

I made my way upstairs through the Daweses' clean, comfortable house. Caitlin's bedroom door was slightly ajar. I slipped inside without disturbing her—she saw me, but she didn't even pause in her playing.

Caitlin was sitting in the hard-backed chair she always used for practicing, right underneath a big framed poster of Beethoven. I sat on her bed, as I did whenever I caught her busy with her cello. Caitlin's room was pretty cool—not too girly-girly, which was one of the reasons I liked it. It was big, with two enormous windows facing her backyard and a padded window seat underneath them. The walls were painted a deep forest green—her favorite color—and the bedspread, lamps, and carpet were all this rich honey tone. One wall was entirely a bookshelf, and near that was a desk piled with papers and a computer. The room was cluttered and a little dark but warm and cozy for its size.

I settled back onto her big, overstuffed pillows as I listened. I didn't know the piece or the composer, but as I closed my eyes to listen I couldn't help wondering if the composer had meant for this piece of music to sound so forlorn.

Not that her playing wasn't beautiful. But today it sounded melancholy and painful somehow. Short, jagged stretches of staccato pins and needles were followed by longer, tortured passages that reminded me of wandering lost in the woods. It felt claustrophobic and a little scary. And yet, for all the sharp edges of the song, Caitlin never let it stop being lovely to listen to.

Finally she dragged to a halt. After a moment of silence I opened my eyes and smiled at her. She looked tired, but also more beautiful to me than anything I'd ever seen. "That was amazing," I told her. "Who was it?"

Caitlin shook her head slightly, as if to clear away the remaining strains of the music. "Brahms," she said. "That one's tricky. But I'll get it down."

"You're close, I can tell." I sat up on the edge of her bed. "How are you feeling? Better?"

She shrugged. "I guess," she replied, looking down at her strings. "I'm okay. Playing always makes me feel better. I'm fine."

I wanted to believe her. In her bedroom that evening, I did try to believe her.

But deep down in my heart I knew she was lying.

Eleven

WE ARRIVED AT the rave in Ryan's minivan just after midnight. The ride up to
the foothills had been raucous—the whole
group of us singing along with the radio, laughing, yelling, and chatting, everybody in wild
moods. The minivan was big, but we were
pretty crammed with all the music equipment.
Besides Ryan, who was driving, and Caitlin and
me, there was Beth, Kenny, Jeff, Andre, and a
blond girl Andre had brought named Melissa.

By the time we arrived, there was a long
line of cars on the dirt road leading to the rave.
Ryan drove us up to a vast meadow, where
parking attendants were organizing all the ve-
hicles into neat rows. As we all climbed out of
the minivan Kenny let out a yelp. "Last chance
to pick your nose!" he called.

Caitlin whacked him on the shoulder. "Gross!"

I hugged Caitlin and shook my head, laughing. I was grateful she seemed to be feeling better. I'd been on her about taking her headache pills—it seemed like they were working.

We lugged our equipment down a long dark path toward a distant glare of colored lights. The moon was a bright silver, and the crowd looked cool and mysterious in the silvery illumination.

Caitlin put her hand on my stomach. "Look up," she whispered.

I did. "Wow," I said in awe. Away from the lights of Boulder, up this high in the mountains where the air was thinner, there was nothing to block our view of the universe in the cloudless sky. I wasn't sure if I'd ever seen so many stars. The night was thick with them, a dazzling spread of brilliant specks. I could even see the tiny ones clustered behind the constellations. I could believe that the sky went on forever.

Leaning over to Caitlin, I kissed her sweet mouth. What else was there to do when you were confronted by the infinite universe besides kiss your girlfriend?

We passed by a flashing police car and an ambulance at the intersection where the dirt path met the main road. Then we were at the rave. An enormous tent revealed itself as we came over a small hill, and I heard the first blast of music.

The beat thrummed up my legs, swelling in my chest. Weird, high-pitched bleeps and sirens echoed over the hills, along with a sinuous keyboard line, chanted vocals, and the call-and-response cheers of the crowd. I couldn't help grinning. Man, was I psyched!

"Stay together!" Jeff called as we headed toward the tent.

We pushed through a dense throng of funkily dressed kids. It would be easy to lose each other. Caitlin held on to the back of my silver shirt as we made our way to the main entrance of the tent.

Standing right outside the big flaps of the entrance was Duane, looking as old and emotionless as always. But even though he looked out of place among all the kids, the way everyone revolved around him let you know exactly who was running the show. That and his clipboard and flashlight.

I jogged over to him. "We're here," I said, unable to contain the excitement in my voice. "Tomorrowland. At your service."

Duane nodded and flipped a page on his clipboard. "Good," he grunted. "Listen, Myers. Do me a favor, right? Backward Evolution flaked on me. Can you guys be set up in a half hour?"

I turned to Ryan and Jeff. "Can we?" I asked.

Ryan shrugged. "I don't see why not."

"The sooner the better," Kenny piped up from behind me.

"Absolutely," I told Duane. "Our pleasure."

We worked out with Caitlin, Beth, and Melissa where we'd meet them after the set, then they took off. The next half hour was a blur of activity. Ryan thought for a few minutes that he'd forgotten one of his cords, but he then located it. Setting up an electronica band was always a technical nightmare—we had tons of cords and plugs and wires to worry about—but Ryan's temporary crisis was the only one we suffered.

Before I even had time to think about it, the band ahead of us was clearing off the stage and we were headed out. I quickly checked my outfit. I was wearing heavy, dark red sneakers, superbaggy, red-dyed jeans, my shimmery silver shirt, and a tall, slouchy, crushed velvet, dark green hat. I was ready.

We stepped out into the flashing, blinking multicolored lights of the stage. The dance floor was open to the sky, nestled in a natural amphitheater between the line of trees on the left and a jagged jut of exposed rocks to the right. It was packed with a mass of heads and faces, all waiting to be turned on by our sound, waiting to get down. I took a deep breath and carried my keyboard to the front of the stage while roadies helped us lug our amps and plug into the sound system as quickly as we could.

The instant Kenny started the opening tones of "Sway," I stopped thinking. Jeff's drumming joined Ryan's rhythm samples and Andre's bass kicked in, and the crowd started to *throb*. This huge wave of humanity jiggled and jangled, spread out before me, but somehow they were all connected—to one another and to us. As our music swelled, ripples ran through the dancing crowd. The crowd had become a single creature moving to our music, a great beast only semitamed by our sound.

I remember feeling pleased at the way my voice sounded as I chanted the song's single lyrical line. I had picked a phrase that seemed sort of meaningless at first, but as I chanted it over and over it picked up meanings, nuances, a whole life of its own.

Caitlin had given me the first part of the line from one of her favorite books, Francesca Lia Block's *Weetzie Bat*.

"Love's a dangerous angel," I sang, "and we're under its sway."

That was the only line in the song. For a good ten minutes I sang it, chanting that line in every possible way. The music behind me slowed, and I murmured it low. Jeff accelerated the rhythm, and I chanted it fast, as a command to dance. Kenny and I both brought the melodies up to a fever pitch, and I sang it high, teetering on the edge of my vocal range, Andre's bass stepped up to front and center, and I whispered sadly. When that petered out, Ryan's samples took over, wordless foreign voices calling out. I got goose bumps up my bare arms as we blew the crowd away.

We worked our way through five songs, ending with "Continental Divide." When the last deeply resonant, buzzing notes of Kenny's didgeridoo faded away, I stood motionless in the sudden silence in the dark and lovely mountains, the light from the stars tickling my face and outstretched arms.

"Thank you!" I called into the crowd. "We're Tomorrowland! And we love you all!"

The returned roar was immensely satisfying—I felt like I was on top of the world.

As I carried my keyboard off the stage I knew that it was Caitlin who had given me the ability to feel the music so strongly. Caitlin had taught me to feel my emotions.

This night was hers.

As quickly as I could I packed away my

equipment. The guys were subdued—even Kenny was quiet, as if he was too happy to speak. I gave them each a quick high five, then hurried into the crowd to find Caitlin.

Before I even spotted her, I heard her call my name.

"Brad!" she yelled, and her arms were around me, and I was rocking with her, my mouth pressed deeply against her neck, inhaling the wonderful scent of her hair. I pulled away for a moment to kiss her—the most sweet, passionate, perfect kiss.

"You were so great, I can't even tell you," Caitlin murmured when we stopped kissing. "They loved you out there; they *loved* you."

"I don't care about them," I said, gazing into her deep brown eyes. "I only care about you. Tell me you love me."

"You know I do."

"Say the words."

"I love you," she whispered, and ducked her head, a deep blush flooding her cheeks. That was the gesture that had first caused me to fall in love with her, and now I felt that warmth again, a thousand times more.

"Every note was for you," I told her. "Every note was *about* you. Do you know how much I love you?"

"I do," she said.

I hugged her again, and for a long time we

just stood there, holding each other in silence.

A few minutes later the music started up again—a new band. "Let's dance," Caitlin insisted, and I let her lead me into the dense throng of shimmying ravers. We pressed up against each other, so tight it was as though we'd never let go. We just swayed in each other's arms.

I saw Jeff and Kenny boogying beside us, lost in the music. Next to them were Andre and Melissa, and on the other side of us were Ryan and Beth. All of us had huge smiles plastered on our faces. We all danced with each other a bit, but mostly I held Caitlin, never wanting to let go. Caitlin had her head against my chest and we were turning in circles, swaying to the music, for what seemed like hours.

Until all of a sudden, out of nowhere, I felt Caitlin go limp in my arms. Her head flopped back and she parted her mouth, uttering a deep, painful moan that froze my heart. Her eyes rolled up, showing only white.

I struggled to hold her up. *"Caitlin,"* I gasped. "What—"

Her hand curled up and beat weakly in the air, then fell limply at her side. I couldn't support her sudden weight, and as gently as I could I lowered her to the ground, my brain screaming with terror.

Blindly I pushed at the legs of the dancers

around us, forcing them to give her room. "Something's wrong!" I cried. "Help! Help me!"

Beth was the first one to kneel by my side. "Is she breathing?" Beth demanded.

I leaned my face down to Caitlin's. I nearly wept with relief when I felt air coming from her lips—it was ragged and slow. "Yes," I said, my voice shaking. "She's breathing. What's the matter with her? *What's the matter with her?*"

"I don't know," Beth told me, her voice scared. "We'd better get her out of here."

"Get an ambulance!" I screamed in a raw howl. *"Get the ambulance here now!"*

Twelve

"**B**RAD?" JEFF SAID. "We're gonna take off, man."

Slowly I glanced up to see my best friends standing in front of me. They all had their jackets on. The truth was, I'd almost forgotten they were here with me. I'd been staring at the tile floor of the hospital waiting room for what felt like days.

"Wh-what time is it?" I croaked.

"Ten A.M.," Beth said.

I stared at her numbly. It had been eight hours since we got here, eight hours since I'd seen Caitlin or even heard anything about her.

"We've got to go home," Beth went on. "But I'll be back this afternoon, okay? Do you want me to bring you anything?"

I shook my head.

"Maybe she'll be able to go home by this afternoon," Becca put in. I glanced over at her. Caitlin's sister sat in the hard plastic seat next to mine, her arms wrapped around her chest. She didn't even look up—it was as if she were talking to herself. I could tell she didn't really believe Caitlin would go home today. She was just trying to keep a positive attitude.

Jeff leaned down to give me a sort of half hug. He smiled at Becca. "I'm sure you're right," he said. "Caitlin will be fine."

The others nodded in agreement. But their words meant nothing to me. The only person I would believe was the tall, silver-haired doctor who had taken Caitlin away. When he said Caitlin was okay, I'd believe him.

Mr. and Mrs. Dawes were in his office right now. They were finding out what was wrong with Caitlin right now. I drew in a shuddering breath. I'd been here all night, but no one would tell me about Caitlin. No one would answer my questions. And even after her family got here, nobody would tell us anything except that Caitlin was having "tests."

What kind of tests? I wondered. Caitlin had never even regained consciousness on the way to the hospital. Where was she now? What was happening to her?

Becca shifted beside me, pushing back her

long dark hair, so much like Caitlin's. I looked up again and realized my friends were gone. I hadn't even noticed them leaving. For all I knew, they might have said good-bye three hours ago—somehow I couldn't seem to keep track of time here. It was as if the hospital was in some different dimension from the outside world.

"They've been in there for half an hour," Becca murmured. "What's taking so long?"

Her voice sounded shaky and frightened. I reached over and took her hand.

Suddenly the door at the end of the hall opened. Caitlin's parents appeared. Mr. Dawes's face was as gray as his sweatshirt. And Mrs. Dawes was sobbing. Crying so hard she could barely walk. Her husband kept his arm around her, steering her slowly down the hall.

Becca gripped my hand, holding it much too tightly, but I didn't care. The pain felt good—physical and small, something I could handle. My pulse pounded in my ears, and it was hard to breathe.

Mr. Dawes led his wife over to us. She didn't stop weeping as he sat her down in the chair beside me. She slumped over and shook with sobs against my arm.

I stared up at Mr. Dawes. His eyes were red and fixed on the wall above my head. I desperately wanted to know what was wrong yet couldn't bring myself to ask.

"Dad," Becca said. Her voice was calm. But her hand still clutched mine tightly.

Mr. Dawes shook his head. He closed his eyes and swayed for a moment where he stood. "I don't . . . ," he murmured. "I don't think I can tell you."

"Dad," Becca began again. She raised the hand she held in mine. "Dad, we need to know."

He nodded and opened his eyes.

"The doctor says . . . he says Caitlin has something called glio . . . glioblastoma multi . . . multi something. Glioblastoma multiforme. I think I have that right." He paused for a long moment and stared down at the ground, then lifted his swollen red eyes up again. He wasn't looking at Becca or me, though—he seemed to be looking past us, as if his gaze could penetrate the wall. "The doctor said it's rare in girls her age, which is why it wasn't diagnosed. It's . . . a kind of cancer. It's cancer. Caitlin . . . she has a big tumor growing from her brain stem, the place where her brain meets her spinal cord. It's fast growing, malignant. They . . . they can't operate. There's nothing they can do for her."

As I stared numbly up at Mr. Dawes his robotic voice finally broke. "Oh, God," he keened. "There's nothing they can do." He leaned forward as though he was going to fall, stopped himself by taking a step. He blinked once, as if he were realizing where he was, then he quietly sat down next to his wife and folded his hands in his lap. His face went blank.

"Mr. Dawes," I said, although I didn't know where I was getting the strength to speak. "Mr. Dawes, how long did they say she has?"

Mr. Dawes didn't reply. He was gazing out at some invisible spot again.

Becca squeezed my hand, and I squeezed back. She leaned over me toward her father. "Dad," she said in a shaky voice, "Brad asked you a question."

He turned his head to Becca. "A few weeks," he whispered. "Maybe a few days. The doctor said she'll probably go into a coma before then. There's nothing they can do."

Then it finally hit me. Caitlin was going to die.

This was real.

I dropped Becca's hand and fell forward, gasping for air as I put my head between my knees. There was no thought—just biting waves of sheer pain and devastation. Above me, far away, I could hear Becca sniffling, and for a second I felt I was going to throw up. I swallowed hard, turning my face into my knee, breathing into the denim of my jeans.

Caitlin was going to die.

In a few weeks.

In a few *days.*

I could not swallow this. Nobody could expect it of me. How could I possibly feel this, endure this—something so unbearable?

My whole body shook. My heart twisted, my stomach lurched, and I panted for breath. I struggled to regain control. And slowly a feeling of numbness spread through me, overcoming the waves of despair. It seemed that there was no way that this could be happening. As if it was all just a nightmare.

Mrs. Dawes twitched against my shoulder. "We have to tell her," she whispered, her voice sounding disembodied and small. "We have to go in there and tell her the truth. The doctor said she was awake. I'm not going to lie to her. My daughter deserves to know the truth."

Her husband nodded mutely. He reached out his hand, stood up, and helped Mrs. Dawes out of her seat. Then the two of them went to find Caitlin's room. After a moment Becca jumped out of her seat and hurried after them, running to catch up.

I stayed where I was. I couldn't move. I don't know how long I sat there, frozen, staring at the toothpaste blue wall in front of me. It could have been two minutes, it could have been two days. I just sat there in my ridiculous, pathetic rave clothes and stared.

Eventually Mrs. Dawes wandered out to the waiting area again. She had an odd sort of pinched look in her eyes. "Brad, honey, she wants to see you," she told me softly.

"I don't know if I can," I said.

"She wants to see you," Mrs. Dawes repeated. "She asked to see you." She reached out and pulled on my arm.

I stood up and allowed her to lead me down the hall. Amazingly I could still walk.

When we reached room 24, Mrs. Dawes opened the door and leaned inside. "Let's give Brad a few minutes alone," she told Becca and her husband in a vacant voice. "I'm sure they want a few minutes alone together."

Becca and Mr. Dawes nodded. They slipped out of the room and moved into the hallway. Mrs. Dawes gave me a little push, and I stepped inside. She closed the door behind me.

For a second I had to fight the urge to turn around, yank open the door, and run for it. I didn't know if I could bear looking at her face, looking into her eyes, knowing that she was going to die.

But this was Caitlin. Caitlin. For her I had to be brave.

I glanced at her.

She was lying in the hospital bed, her chestnut

hair spread out behind her on the pillow. Caitlin looked tired and worn-out . . . but she was still my girlfriend, the most beautiful girl in the world. "Hi," I said.

"You look awfully stiff and . . . *formal,*" Caitlin told me weakly. She laughed. "Brad, it's just me. I feel okay."

"That's good," I murmured, staring down at the floor.

Caitlin struggled to sit up. "Look at me," she insisted. "*Look* at me."

I stared directly into her deep brown eyes.

She smiled. "Brad, don't try to pretend you don't feel anything because I know you do. I *know* you; I know your tricks. So don't even try it."

At the sound of her voice, the weight of her words, hot tears burst from my eyes and flowed down my cheeks. I gasped and rushed to her side, easing myself down on the edge of the bed beside her. "I—I—I . . . ," I sputtered, "Cait-Caitlin, I—"

"Just go ahead and cry," she told me with a sniffle. "You'll feel better."

I reached out for her hand and held it gently as hot, suffocating tears rushed down my face. She was crying too—I could hear her sobs as my own weeping brought my head down closer and closer to her chest.

Then suddenly Caitlin shoved my head

away and completely lost control. She slammed her fists down on the sides of the bed, pounding the mattress. She shook her shoulders and flailed her head, bucking and screaming. For a split second I thought she was having some sort of seizure. I almost ran for the doctor. But her eyes were awake and conscious—and filled with rage.

"Hey, *hey,*" I said, reaching out for her. As soon as my hands touched her she crumpled up and lay down, panting. I stroked her shoulders and her hair. "I'm here," I whispered, calming her.

"It's so *unfair,*" she cried, covering her eyes with her arm. "Why me? Why am *I* going to die? I . . . I'm only sixteen! I'll never get to play onstage at the Met, I'll never—" She broke off as deep, wet sobs overcame her.

I ran my hand along her cheek. I could hardly bear to watch her like that. Again part of me wanted to run away, unable to deal.

But I stayed right where I was, stroking her cheek. This was Caitlin. And for her sake I'd face anything. Anything at all.

"It's *not* fair," I whispered. "It's not. If I could take this from you, I would. I love you, I love you more than anything in the world. And I'll be right here with you, every step of the way. I'll be here throughout whatever you have to face."

Caitlin grabbed my arm. She looked at me with those swirling, dangerous brown eyes of hers. "You will?" she asked.

"I will," I promised.

She exhaled a deep breath. "Thank you," she said. "Thank you."

Before I could think of what I should be saying to her, I started to say what was on my mind. "But I don't know—"

"What?"

I hesitated. I couldn't share this with Caitlin—I had to be strong for her.

"Tell me," Caitlin insisted. "Just tell me, Brad."

I shook my head, angry at myself. "It's just that," I began finally, "it's just that I'm afraid. I don't know. . . . I'm not sure I'll be able to *handle* . . . everything. I'm not good at that. I can't ask you to help me, I *know* that . . . but you, you're all I've got, and I don't know where else to turn—I don't know how to deal with this. . . ."

Caitlin reached out and placed the palm of her hand against my cheek, rubbing her thumb against my salty-tear lips—just like she had on our first date. "I think . . . ," she told me, "I think that we have to realize that the *point* of life is love. And I know I love you. Just . . . just remember that love includes sadness. It's *part* of it, and it's part of life."

I nodded, tears streaming down my face once more.

"We need to remember that," she whispered.

I pressed my hand to hers on my cheek, and we sat there for a long, lingering moment, just together.

"Brad, will you hold me?" Caitlin asked, breaking our silence.

And I did.

Thirteen

"**B**RAD, TELL CAITLIN I stopped by, okay?" Beth asked a week later. She kept her voice down, even though we were in the hallway outside Caitlin's room. "I don't want to wake her."

I nodded. Beth had come to the hospital almost every day, sometimes bringing Ryan with her. And Becca and Mrs. Dawes were here all the time, of course. Mr. Dawes still went to work during the days—he had decided not to take time off. We all knew that work was the one thing keeping him sane. He was a good guy, but he was definitely becoming stiffer and more distant as Caitlin deteriorated. I couldn't blame him. Everyone had their own ways of dealing.

I dealt by never leaving the hospital—I only

went home for an hour a day to shower and change. I had told my mom what was going on with Caitlin, and she must have called the school because no one had bugged me about not being there. She tried to get me to tell her more about the situation, but I made it clear that she was the last person I wanted to talk to. Besides, I didn't have the time. I spent every minute with Caitlin, helping her eat, making fun of bad daytime television together, playing cards, and talking. Sometimes we just sat together in silence, and that was good too.

"The guys all said to send their best," Beth continued, cutting in on my thoughts. "Everybody's worried about you too, Brad. You should try to get some sleep."

"She's right," Mrs. Dawes said, coming out of Caitlin's room and quietly closing the door behind her. "You should go home and get a good night's sleep."

"But—," I began.

"You can't be strong for Caitlin if you're ready to collapse from exhaustion," Mrs. Dawes interrupted. "And I'm sure your mother is worried about you."

I doubt it, I thought. But Mrs. Dawes had a good point about being strong for Caitlin.

"Okay," I said. "But I'll be back first thing in the morning."

★　　★　　★

170

"You're crazy," Becca told me a few days later. "Peanuts is way cooler than Calvin and Hobbes."

"Oh, come on," I scoffed. "How can you even say that?"

"She's right," Caitlin put in, her voice sounding stronger than it had all day. I'd noticed that Becca had that effect on her. Whenever Caitlin seemed depressed, Becca would start arguing with her or with me. And it always worked—Caitlin would grow excited, her intense eyes flashing as she made her points. I knew Becca was doing it on purpose, and I began to love her like a sister despite her prickly, bossy side. She never wallowed in misery but kept strong, and I respected that.

Becca went to school every day, but I couldn't. I didn't care if I got into trouble or if I fell behind. School seemed like part of another life, a distant dream. I simply wasn't going to leave Caitlin's side one second longer than I had to.

I bounced a little on the end of Caitlin's hospital bed. "Aren't you supposed to be on *my* side?" I teased her.

Caitlin grinned, her eyes lighting up in her pale, pale face.

"Not when you're saying something stupid," she teased back. "Peanuts has so many more levels than Calvin and Hobbes. It's much deeper."

I shook my head. "But Calvin is funnier."

"When Calvin has been around as long as Peanuts, then you can compare them," Becca put in. "Peanuts has been going for nearly fifty years, and it's still great."

"You just like it because you're so much like Lucy," I shot back.

Caitlin laughed, and Becca stuck out her tongue at me.

At times like these it was hard to believe that Caitlin wouldn't get better. But then there were the other times. The times when Caitlin's pain was so bad that she would just lie in bed and sob. The times when her eyes would glaze over with exhaustion and she'd sink into sleep right in the middle of a conversation.

I saw an X ray of the tumor once. On the blue-black transparency the nasty thing looked like a small, vile gourd wrapped around the base of her brain. Caitlin's pain was caused by the pressure built up in her skull as the tumor fought for room, crushing her brain. I hated that tumor more than anything. Sometimes when Caitlin slept, I waved my hands over her, wishing I could draw the tumor out of her and into myself. I concentrated as deeply as I could and imagined it being sucked out of her through the air and into my hands. But each daily X ray or CAT scan only showed that it had grown larger.

Day by day, Caitlin's motor functions disintegrated. The tiny tremor I'd noticed in her hand at the picnic months ago was now constant and unstoppable as the tumor continued to press against her spinal cord and brain stem. Her eyelids twitched and fluttered constantly, and sometimes her whole head would give this awful jerk—as though a spider had crawled up her back.

But even with her face twisted in agony, her arms and legs racked with spasms, and her body tensed as though it would suddenly crumple, I only loved her more. Of course it was her beauty that had first attracted me to her—that and the bright spark in her deep brown eyes—but those things weren't important anymore. Now I truly believed that we were two halves of the same whole.

One day, around two weeks after she'd first been admitted to the hospital, we were alone. It was the middle of the afternoon, and old *Saturday Night Live* reruns were on Comedy Central, but we weren't watching the television that closely. I was sitting in the chair beside Caitlin, just sort of being there for her. By that point that was all Caitlin wanted or needed.

Caitlin turned to me. "Brad?"

"Yes?" I leaned forward in my chair.

She licked her lips. "You keep your heart

open, okay?" she whispered. "No matter what, you do that. Okay? That's . . . important. You go on with your life."

Then she closed her eyes. And slept.

I stared blankly at her for a long moment, the sound of my blood rushing in my ears. "Caitlin?" I asked. "Caitlin?"

No reply.

I shook her gently, calling her name again. My heart was pounding furiously. I was certain she was gone, and I started to shake my head, *No, no, no . . .*

Then, with a sudden burst of relief, I realized her heart monitor was still beeping regularly. I let out a long breath as I listened to it. She was still here—she was just sleeping. I noticed the rate of the beeping heart monitor was gently slowing.

I jumped to my feet and ran to the door. I glanced wildly around the hallway, shouting, "Help! We need a doctor in here!"

A nurse ran down the hall toward the main station. A second later a voice over the loud-speaker ordered doctors to go to room 24. And a few minutes after that I was pushed out of the way as two doctors and a nurse rushed into the room.

"She's not breathing," one doctor warned.

I watched, my back against the wall beside the door, as they snaked a tube down her throat and made a machine breathe for her. My shoulders shaking, I watched them fuss over her for a long time. I didn't move from my place against the wall.

Finally the doctors seemed to agree that they'd stabilized her. They'd hooked her up to a complicated array of tubes and wires, all meant to keep her body alive as the tumor rapidly squashed her brain. I had a sudden, terrible urge to run over and rip out all the tubes, freeing her from the machines. But that insane thought passed almost as quickly as it came.

I jumped a little as Mrs. Dawes stepped into the room. She dropped the cup of coffee she'd been holding, and it splashed against her legs. "Wha . . . what's going on?"

A doctor turned to face her and took a deep breath. "As we explained might happen, Caitlin's slipped into a coma," he told her softly. "We'll do everything to make her as comfortable as possible."

Mrs. Dawes stared back at the doctor. "Is there . . . is there anything I can—" She broke off her sentence and took my hand. "Is there anything *we* can do?"

I slipped my arm around her shoulders.

The doctor nodded. "You probably should continue as you've been doing," he explained. "Many studies indicate that coma patients can hear the voices of their loved ones, perhaps even feel their touch. Your support can only help."

Coma, I thought. We'd never hear Caitlin speak again. We wouldn't even be able to know if she was trying to communicate with us.

I dropped my head and let the tears fall down my cheeks.

"Sorry to wake you." The nurse's voice floated into my ears. "But it's time to change her IV bag."

I nodded groggily and pulled my chair away from Caitlin's bed so the nurse could reach the IV.

"Is it morning yet?" I asked.

"Two o'clock in the morning," the nurse answered.

I yawned. I hadn't gone home to sleep in days, not since Caitlin went into the coma. Neither had Mrs. Dawes—I could hear her slow breathing now as she slept on the cot across the room. I just couldn't go home; I couldn't leave Caitlin. She needed me more than ever. I knew she was there, trapped in her own head, lost in the dark. I did anything I could to reach her and let her know that she was loved.

I played music for her, I read books to her, I held her hand—all the time watching for a sign that she'd returned to me, watching for any flicker of life.

"All finished," the nurse said, giving me a sympathetic smile as she padded out of the room. I pulled my chair back over to the bed so I was only a few inches from Caitlin's beautiful face.

I took her hand. "I love you, Cait," I whispered. "You're the most important thing in my world. I didn't even know it was possible to feel this way about another human being."

I swallowed down the lump in my throat. "I know you're fighting," I went on, keeping my voice quiet so I didn't wake Mrs. Dawes. "I know you're trying to come back to me. Please come back. I miss you so much . . . so much it aches."

A single tear fell from my eye and landed on Caitlin's pillow. I'd lost track of how many times I'd said things like this to her. It was all I could do—tell her how much she meant to me, how much her love had changed my life and made me happy. Sometimes, when I was certain nobody was looking, I kissed her. I kissed her with all the love and passion I held, hoping that it would be enough to break Sleeping Beauty's spell of eternal sleep.

But she never stirred.

"How is she?" I asked at about ten o'clock the next night.

The young doctor glanced over at me, as if

she was surprised to see me there. "Stable," she answered. "No change."

I stared back, not answering. The heart monitor went on beeping like it always did. How I hated that sound. How I hated the whole *hospital.* I hated the clean, sterile rooms and halls, the smell of disinfectant heavy in the air. And I especially hated the doctors who couldn't do anything to save Caitlin.

Doctors like this one, who didn't even know Caitlin. Doctors who just came in, shook their heads, and said, "No change. Stable, but no change."

No change.

The doctor walked out of the room, leaving me alone with Caitlin, alone with the beeping of the machines. Suddenly I couldn't take it for one second longer. It was driving me crazy. *No change, no change, no change.* No matter how much I loved Caitlin, no matter how desperately I wanted everything to be all right, that heart monitor kept up its steady, constant beeping. *No change.*

I jumped up and walked out of the room, away from Caitlin and the horrifying machines that she needed to sustain her life. I wandered into the lobby and found Mrs. Dawes in the waiting room, dozing on a bench. I woke her gently, and with only a nod she understood I wanted to switch shifts with her.

All I did was go get a soda. I just needed a short break. I drank the soda, threw the can into the recycling bin, and headed back toward room 24.

But as I approached, it dawned on me that the room was too quiet.

I couldn't hear the beeping of the machines.

I took off running down the hall, skidding slightly as I made the turn into Caitlin's room.

Mrs. Dawes was sitting beside Caitlin on the bed, humming softly as she stroked Caitlin's long, chestnut hair. The heart monitor beside the bed was dark.

I stood in the doorway, my heart hammering in my chest, until Mrs. Dawes glanced up at me.

"Th-the machine," I stuttered. "It's not—"

"I turned it off," Mrs. Dawes told me quietly. "It went flat line, and I turned it off. I don't know if that's allowed, but it doesn't matter, does it? It doesn't matter."

I couldn't move. My lips parted, and I made a tiny little moan.

"She just slipped away," she murmured. "I was sitting right here, and she just slipped away. A simple, silent passage . . ." Her hand froze above Caitlin's hair midstroke. "She's gone. My little girl is gone."

I could only stare as Mrs. Dawes bowed her head and began to weep. All around me the room itself seemed to tremble, and the walls wavered as though I was looking at the whole scene through the heat haze on a highway.

Caitlin had pulled away from us; she had pulled away from me. Too far away for me to reach. She had dived downstream from the Continental Divide, flowing forever away from me, flowing west, straight on till sunset.

And never again would our streams flow together.

Tears streaking down my face, I ran out of the room and fled the hospital, the hospital in which Caitlin had died.

Fourteen

*B*RAD, YOU LEFT me, the pink blossom murmured as it tumbled into the darkness. I reached out to grab it, to save it, to bring it back to me, but it fell farther out of reach of my grasping fingers. Petals shimmering like starlight dwindled into the inky black night.

Brad, I heard it whimper, *you left me to die without you beside me—*

I sat up straight in bed, my heart pounding, my face and the back of my neck glazed with cold sweat.

A dream. A *nightmare.* Again.

I collapsed back against my bed, taking deep breaths as I waited for my heartbeat to return to normal. In the ten days since Caitlin had died, sleep had not been easy. That's an

181

understatement. Sleep had been impossible.

Late afternoon sunlight streamed around the edges of my curtains, its rays flat and gray. I hadn't been out of bed for a long time, since Caitlin's funeral. I ached all over, my arms twinged with sorrow, and I felt cold deep in the marrow of my bones.

Even music sounded distant and drab. Early that morning I'd gotten up and slipped on my headphones, hoping that playing a song would remind me of something good. But that had been a waste of time and left me feeling worse than before. Each note I played sounded tinny and far away, as though I was hearing it through an ancient radio. I'd quickly returned to bed, where I'd stayed for the rest of the day.

I covered my eyes with the crook of my arm. I felt as though every limb of my body weighed a thousand pounds. Why had I ever allowed myself to fall in love with Caitlin? This aching hole in my chest would never heal.

I lowered my arm and opened my eyes as I heard my bedroom door creak. My mother stood in the doorway with a tray of food.

"Go away," I whispered. I didn't want to see *anybody,* but she wasn't even on the list of remote possibilities.

My mother pursed her lips and walked inside anyway. She set the tray down on my bedside table and sat next to me on the bed.

"I brought you some lunch," she said. "A turkey sandwich, some grape juice, and a couple of peanut butter cookies. You really should eat something."

My stomach clenched at the thought.

"It's with mayo and lettuce, on toasted wheat bread," my mother tried again.

That was usually my favorite. But it was the favorite sandwich of a different Brad, a Brad who hadn't known what misery really was.

"Brad, you need to eat," my mother said. She was starting to sound nervous.

Why wouldn't she just go away? Didn't she know that Caitlin was dead? I held myself perfectly still, hoping that my mother would get the hint and leave me be.

She sighed. "Are you okay?"

I blinked at her. "Am I *okay?*" I shot back in disbelief. "Of course I'm not okay! Caitlin is *dead.*" I turned my head to stare at the ceiling.

"Do you want to talk about it?" she asked, her voice shaking.

Letting out a little gasp of frustration, I closed my eyes. *Did I want to talk about it?* This question from the woman whom I hadn't spoken to in months, who hated Caitlin, who tried to get me to spend less time with her? And now she asked me if I wanted to *talk about it?*

I clenched my hands into fists, fury rising

within me. I popped open my eyes and glared at her.

There was sympathy in my mother's eyes—sympathy she didn't deserve to feel.

I slammed my fists down at my sides, thumping the bed hard. "So you were right!" I screamed at her. "So you were right all along! I *should* have been more careful, protected myself just like you do! I *should* have broken up with Caitlin before I got in too deep—"

"No, no—," my mother protested.

"So now what?" I spat out. "So now what do you want? To tell me 'I told you so'?"

My mother dropped her hands into her lap, staring at me in shock. Her mouth twitched for a moment, then her whole face went blank and expressionless. Without another word she slowly rose from my bed and walked out of the room.

"And stay out!" I called after her.

I burst into tears as I heard her climb the stairs, and I turned over into a fetal position, curling my hands under my pillow.

Oh, Caitlin, I thought. *Why did you leave me? Don't you know how much I miss you? Don't you know how empty I feel without you—*

No, I told myself viciously. *No. Don't.*

My mother *had* been right. She'd been trying to teach me a painful lesson that she herself had learned, and I'd been too blind with love to listen.

I would never, ever let myself fall into that trap again. I would never let myself care about anyone again. The results were just too painful.

Because love doesn't last. Love dies.

The following Monday I went back to school. I was pretty far behind since I'd missed nearly three weeks of classes, but none of the teachers gave me a hard time. They all knew what had happened.

By the time I was sitting at my desk in third period—history—I was fed up with the pitying looks everyone had been giving me. Even when I bumped into Jeff in the hallway and he promised me his support, I felt annoyed. I just couldn't stand the fact that all these people—both friends and strangers—could so easily read how deeply I was hurting.

Ms. Korman was writing a list of the causes of the French Revolution up on the blackboard, but I couldn't concentrate. School still seemed too far outside myself—like I wasn't even really there. What *was* real was the longing that battered my heart.

Two seats ahead to my left Sue Hallford, a girl I'd spoken to maybe six times at most, turned around to glance at me. This look of horrible pity was heavy in her eyes. I quickly looked away and stared down at my open notebook, forcing the few notes I'd taken to glaze up unfocused in my vision.

Stay cool, I commanded myself. *You can handle this. You can get through today.*

Suddenly I felt close to tears. My hand holding my pen started to shake, and I gripped my wrist with my other hand, trying to calm myself down.

Then my stomach turned over, and for a second I thought I was going to be sick. I closed my eyes until the nausea passed, trying to keep my breathing as even as possible.

But I still felt awful. When the bell rang, instead of heading to chemistry I walked out of school and drove home. I was not ready to face a whole day of school, that much was obvious.

When I got home, I was surprised to find my mother's car in the driveway. She *never* missed a day of work. I parked behind her and headed inside. I was curious as to what she was doing home, but I certainly wasn't planning on asking her about it.

I stopped short when I entered the living room and saw her slumped on the couch, her head in her hands. She held a tissue up to her nose, and there were crumpled rosebuds of used tissues beside her on the couch.

She was crying. My mother *never* cried. I hadn't seen her shed a tear once since my father had left, not even at Caitlin's funeral. Just seeing her like that made my hands start to tremble.

She looked up as I entered. Her face was red and blotchy, her eyes puffy. "Oh, Brad—," she began tearfully.

I gave a little groan and stalked past her quickly, starting to run only when I had made it clear of the living room. I bolted down to my room and shut the door.

After dropping my backpack in the corner, I shucked off my sneakers and climbed into bed. I needed to escape, and sleep was the only way to do it. That is, if I didn't have another nightmare.

Then the door to my bedroom opened. My mother had dried her eyes a bit, although she still held a tissue in her hand.

"What?" I asked, crossing my arms over my chest.

She curled her hand around the edge of the door, swinging it slightly. "You came home from school early?"

"You came home from work early?" I returned, mimicking her tone exactly.

My mother nodded and sniffled. "I wasn't feeling well. I wasn't . . . feeling right."

I arched my eyebrows. "I didn't know you *could* feel."

She shook her head and walked into my

room, easing herself down on the end of my bed. I pulled my legs up, bending my knees, shifting away from her.

"I deserve that," she told me. She looked down at her hands, her back turned to me.

I didn't know what to do. I'd never seen my mother looking so . . . vulnerable—at least not in the past few years. It made me feel awkward. She'd been so consistent for so long, and now that was falling apart too.

"I'm not in the mood to talk to anyone—," I began.

"Brad, I'm so sorry," she blurted at almost the same time. Her eyes brimmed with tears again as I circled my knees with my arms.

She swallowed. "I've been feeling sick all weekend, just hating myself for what . . . for what I led you to believe."

"You were right," I whispered.

My mother shook her head vehemently. "No, Brad, I was wrong. Very wrong. I never should have . . . It was terrible of me to do what I did, to tell you to stay away from Caitlin. I never should have done that, dragging my own problems into your life. Taking my own things out on you. Caitlin was a lovely girl—"

"She was," I said. I felt so close to tears. But I pinched the side of my leg, concentrating on the pain, willing myself to hold steady.

With a nod my mother took a deep breath. "I know I've been distant with you, but I never meant for it to get so bad, to become . . ." She sniffled again. "After your father left us—"

"Mom," I whispered. "Don't. You don't have to say anything."

"Yes," she replied. "Yes, I do. My pain is hurting you, and that was never supposed to happen. I thought if I just kept my chin up, didn't let my anger and sadness affect me, and just faced my life, everything . . . well, everything would be manageable. I wanted to be strong for you. Your father and I just never saw eye to eye. That shouldn't have anything to do with you."

"Dad left," I said weakly.

"Because of problems *we* were having," my mother choked out. "Not because of you. Okay? You shouldn't do what I had to do. You shouldn't try to block your emotions out of your life." She wiped her nose with her tissue. "And we were okay for a little while, right?"

She turned to face me, her eyes bleary with tears, and all I could do was nod in agreement.

"Yes, we were okay for a while," she continued, turning back around. "But then we had that fight, which was all my fault, and I started to see that I couldn't get back to the feelings I'd pushed away. I couldn't feel my life anymore, even when you were hurt, even when I needed more than anything in the world to be there for you. . . ."

She let out a little sob, then continued. "Don't let that happen to you," she told me. "It's not right. You need to live your life."

I flinched at the words, a near replica of Caitlin's last words to me. "I'll try," I said, fighting back tears.

"Good," she said, squeezing my shoulder. "Good." Then she let out a big sigh and stood up slowly, looking a lot older than she usually did.

She took a few steps toward the door, then turned back to face me again. "Listen," she said. "I'm still your mother, and I'm so sorry about what's happened between us. I hope you believe that because it's true."

"I believe it," I told her.

"And I just want you to know, whatever help I can give to help you through this, it's yours. Anything I can do."

"Thank you," I said as she left my room, closing the door gently behind her.

I slumped back against the mattress.

Sure, it was good that I was no longer fighting with my mother and that we'd taken steps to close the distance between us.

But Caitlin was still dead, and nothing would change that. No apology from my mother could change the way I felt.

I was too far gone.

Fifteen

O N FRIDAY EVENING a week later my mother opened my door. I was doing my usual—I was curled up in bed with the lights off, watching a rerun of *The Simpsons*.

"I'm not hungry," I told my mother.

"Good," she said. "Because I didn't bring you any food. You've got visitors, Brad."

I snuggled deeper into the sheet that was covering me. "Tell them to go away," I said. "I don't want to see anybody."

"Tough," she replied, and she threw the door wide open and stepped back into the hall.

Jeff, Kenny, Ryan, and Andre shuffled forward nervously, entering my dark room.

I sat up in bed, my heart racing. I didn't even know how to deal with talking to actual living people. Except for my mother, I hadn't seen anyone in a week. I hadn't been to school. The only people I saw were on TV. Day after day I'd stared at the television, waiting for it to take me someplace else, someplace that wasn't nearly so painful.

What else was there to do? Without Caitlin what point was there in doing anything? Without her why should I care about the stuff that happened every day? Without her everything felt worthless.

And my band? Like I could really sing "Continental Divide" after what had happened. Like I could sing anything ever again.

This was my punishment, I thought. My punishment for falling in love with Caitlin. I'd been too happy, I'd trusted in love, and now I had to pay for it by crying myself to sleep every night. In return for thinking I could be blissfully happy, I now had to detach myself from life entirely.

Becca had called, inviting me to have dinner with her parents, but I told her I couldn't handle that yet, and she said she understood. Jeff had stopped by, and Kenny and Ryan, but when I was home by myself, I didn't answer the door, and when my mother was home, I told her to send them away. Why had she let them in now?

"Hey, Brad-man," Jeff said awkwardly.

"Hey," I replied.

They stood silently near the doorway. I could tell they were trying to think of what to say, but I wasn't about to help them out. I didn't care. I didn't even want them there.

The Simpsons came back on, and at the sound of the cartoon's music Kenny rushed over to my bed. "Which one is this?" he demanded, peering at the TV. "When Homer goes into space?"

"No," I responded. "I think it's the one when they go into the witness protection program. Sideshow Bob and the houseboat and all that."

Kenny smiled. "*Love* that one," he said. "The best is when Homer can't remember his new name."

"Yeah," I said flatly. "That's funny."

Since Kenny had broken the ice—or rather, *The Simpsons* had—the rest of the guys trooped into my room. Jeff and Andre settled on my couch, and Ryan sat on the floor at the foot of my bed. With a sigh I struggled to sit up. Obviously they weren't going to leave anytime soon—at least not until the show was over.

We all focused on the television. The guys laughed along, and Kenny recited lines, with Ryan correcting his mistakes. It started to feel okay to have them there. Television was much more interesting when other people were watching it with you.

But a tense silence fell over us at the next commercial. They—except Kenny, who still seemed fascinated with the TV—were obviously searching for something to say to me. The silence thickened until I couldn't take it any longer. I reached out with my remote and turned off the television.

"Hey!" Kenny protested. "I was watching that!"

"Kenny," Ryan said, shaking Kenny's leg, "that's not why we're here, remember?"

"So," I began. "What's up?"

Andre nudged Jeff, and Jeff leaned forward. "Uh, Brad, the guys and I got together and decided to come over, like, as an *intervention*."

Andre and Ryan nodded. Kenny said, "Yeah."

I rolled my eyes. "I'm not on drugs, and I'm not an alcoholic. My problem is that Caitlin is dead."

That shut them up. But not for long.

"We know," Ryan said. "We all loved Caitlin, and her death was tough on everybody. She was the best. I was miserable and crying for days, honestly. And I'm sure the other guys did too—"

"I cried," Andre broke in. "Like a baby."

I felt dangerously near tears. "Look," I said. "I know you guys mean well, but I can't—"

"Brad," Jeff interrupted, "it *sucks* that

Caitlin died. It's like the worst thing ever. And I know, I mean, I'm *guessing* that you don't, you don't know what to live for. I personally have never had a girlfriend. . . ." Jeff's voice trailed off, and he glanced down at his feet. But then he looked up at me again, his eyes serious and sad. "But if I did, and she died, I'm sure that's how I would feel—like it's all over." He sighed. "I guess what I want to say is that we need you too." He turned to the others. "Right, guys?"

"Absolutely," Ryan said.

Kenny nodded. "It's just not the same without you, man."

"We love you," Andre added. "We're a *band.*"

I didn't say anything for a long time, not trusting myself to speak. My friends *were* the best. And it wasn't fair what I'd been doing, removing myself from their lives. I knew they counted on me to lead Tomorrowland. I also knew that in this weird way, the four of them probably wouldn't be friends without me in the center. But how could I explain to them how truly messed up I was? I wasn't sure I'd ever be the old Brad again, that I'd ever feel normal again.

"Thanks," I said, picking at the hem of my pillowcase. "You guys do mean a lot to me. But Caitlin was like my heart, and I—"

"Hey!" Kenny interrupted, a big smile on his face. "You remember way back when, when Caitlin showed up in your driveway and totally chewed you out? You hadn't gone to see her play cello or something—and anyway, she, like, ripped you to shreds. That was an *awesome* thing to watch! I was scared you were going to pass out from shock!"

Ryan and Jeff laughed, and Andre smiled. "She was wild sometimes," Jeff added.

"Yeah," Ryan said. "I remember you told me the story of when you two went skiing in Vail—"

"C'mon, guys," I protested. "I don't feel like thinking about—"

"I could totally picture her dive-bombing to the bottom of the hill," Ryan continued, ignoring me. "You described that so well. She was screaming, 'Look out below!'"

"Out of control," I corrected him, smiling despite myself.

"Yeah," Ryan said. He sat up on the bed beside Kenny. "I love that story—"

"What I remember," Andre said, "was how she could listen."

Ryan shut up immediately. We all turned to stare at Andre.

"What do you mean?" I asked.

Andre shrugged and stretched out his legs in front of him. "Once I was feeling messed up

196

about this fight I had with my dad, and I found Caitlin in Café Roma. She let me tell her all about it, just let me talk. She didn't give advice or anything because she didn't have to. She knew she just had to listen, and I felt better."

That was the longest speech I'd ever heard Andre say. And it was in praise of Caitlin. I couldn't help myself—a tear rolled down my cheek and puddled in the corner of my lips.

I licked it away and sniffled. "She was like that," I told Andre. "But you guys, as much as I appreciate you coming here, you have to give me time, okay? I can't handle . . . remembering her, not yet. But thanks."

"Anytime," Ryan said. "Beth sends her love too."

"Yeah," Kenny added. "Anytime."

"Come back to us soon," Jeff told me. "We need you, Brad-man."

I thanked them again, and one by one they hugged me and left.

When they were gone, I curled back up in bed and I let myself cry.

I hadn't realized just how much my friends had loved Caitlin. Just hearing them talk about her did something to me—it allowed me to breathe a little easier and to feel less alone. I wasn't ready to rejoin the world yet or go back to the band—not even close. But it helped to know that my sadness was shared. Caitlin would never be forgotten. She had touched so many people and had spread so much love.

The world was so much emptier without her.

A few weeks later I was sitting in my room, doing homework. That Monday after the guys came to talk to me, I'd returned to school and it had been okay. Most of my classmates had started to forget about me and my problems—which was absolutely fine with me. I went about business as usual, getting up in the morning, going to school, coming back home to putter around. I managed to pretend I had a normal life.

But I still couldn't handle starting up rehearsals with Tomorrowland again. That would have been too much. Even though I was going through the motions of living, my heart was far from healed. And I was pretty sure it never would be.

I tried to concentrate on my trig homework, but the sines and cosines and all the formulas blurred in my head. Usually I forced myself to stop when I found myself drifting off into memories of Caitlin since coming back to reality afterward was always so painful. But once in a while the memories were so wonderful that I just let myself go. . . .

I floated back to the first time I'd heard

her play her cello, her wonderful music. I could recall sitting in that music room in the September School so vividly, closing my eyes and letting myself sink into the beautiful, lonely colors she'd conjured up in my mind.

I popped my eyes open and gripped my pencil tightly. Her music was lost to me forever. I would never hear her play again or lose myself in the shades of lovely emotion she could bring out in her music. I would have given anything to hear her cello again—

Then it hit me. There was that sample that Ryan had recorded of her playing that time she had come to a Tomorrowland practice.

I still had it—Ryan had given it to me on a tape.

I threw down my pen and rushed over to my stereo system. My equipment was dusty—I'd barely used it in the past month. I blew on it, then quickly located the cassette Ryan had passed along to me.

I opened the tape case so quickly that the cover fell off its little plastic hinges. Then I jammed the cassette into the deck and pressed play.

Caitlin's music softly seeped out into the room. I raised the volume and dropped to my knees, listening with my eyes closed.

It was like she was right there with me

again, her face slack with concentration, bobbing her head as she worked the bow over the strings. All the beautiful colors I remembered were with me as well, spreading and changing into miraculous shapes behind my eyelids. I ached with the power of her emotional, evocative music. My eyes filled with tears, and I let them fall.

There was so much passion, so much love, so much life in her music. Caitlin couldn't really be dead, not if I was experiencing something that was so much a part of her, not if I was listening to every subtlety of her feelings that she expressed in her music.

But she *was* dead. And I had only this recording of her pure music to truly remember her by.

On the tape Caitlin's playing shifted to a sadder passage. She brought me with her as she explored the tiny, dark corners of sadness, the pain and loneliness, the empty longing that she'd never shied away from in life.

That she'd never shied away from in life.

I hugged myself as the sample trailed off. I realized that Caitlin's music often contained sadness. This was what Caitlin had tried to make me understand, that life was just like music—passionate, full of all different emotions . . . of happiness *and* sadness. That was so deeply true, so basic, that I wondered how it had taken me so long to figure it out.

How could I deny the passion I felt with Caitlin? That was like denying *her*. And I could never do that. I had to keep that passion alive.

I wiped away my tears, opened my eyes, and rewound the tape. Then I climbed to my feet and pulled the dust cover off my keyboard. I turned the synth on, pressed play on the tape again, and I was ready.

As the sound of Caitlin's cello filled my bedroom I began to play along, adding my melody to hers. I wasn't sure exactly where the melody I was playing was coming from, but it seemed to be somewhere deep within me, a little quiet corner I'd almost forgotten was there.

I kept up with her, leavening her sad sections with an upbeat phrase, adding depth to her cheerful parts with a touch of melancholy, reminding myself that both exist in equal measure as parts of the same whole.

And I found myself lost in our music, my heart joining with hers once again.

I continued to play for a long time after her sample had run out, my fingers bringing forth a lonely call to her, a promise of love that I would always remember.

But finally I had to wind down. I was exhausted—simply worn out.

And as I rested my hands on my keyboard with my head bowed, I heard a sniffle from behind me.

I turned around and saw my mother leaning in the doorway, tears rolling down her face.

She glanced up, sniffled again, and smiled through her tears. "That was beautiful," she told me. "Just so beautiful."

I couldn't stand her tears. I ran to her. My mother closed her arms around me in a tight hug.

"Mom, I just miss her so much," I sobbed.

"I know," she whispered, her lips pressed gently against the top of my head. "Don't hold that pain inside, Brad. Life's too short." And she just held me as I cried onto her shoulder.

Caitlin would have been so happy to see my mother and me finally reconciled. I owed it all to her.

I still ached with pain and sadness at the thought of Caitlin, but finally I could remember how happy—how truly happy—the love we'd shared had made me.

And I would never forget.

Epilogue

I SIGH AND rub my eyes, blinking into the dim light of the empty tent. I still miss Caitlin. I always will.

The second I notice that the music coming through the tent wall has stopped, Kenny pokes his head through the tent flaps. He searches around for a second and finally locates me in my place in the corner. He gives me a nervous, questioning look, raising his eyebrows.

I smile at him. "I'm okay," I say. "It's time for us to go on, huh?"

"Yeah," he says. "You ready?"

"As I'll ever be," I reply. Of course I have to go on. I can't shut down my life—denying any part of life is just like denying the love I shared with Caitlin. And I'll never do that. No matter what.

Kenny grins at me. "Here we go," he says. Just as he picks up his keyboard Ryan, Jeff, and Andre rush in and motor over to their equipment. Jeff glances at me, and I nod.

The show must go on.

Then before I even know it, we're setting up onstage. When my keyboard is plugged in and ready to go, I shade my eyes with my hand and stare out into the crowd. There seem to be even more ravers out there than the last time, if that's possible. The crowd cheers as I wave.

Standing in front of the audience feels so different this time. It seems like a thousand years have passed since Tomorrowland entertained on this stage, but it's really only been a couple of months. Last time I knew Caitlin would be waiting for me when I finished, and I was filled with the idea that everything was right with the world.

Now I know better. But Caitlin is still with me, because I remember her and will never forget her. With her in my heart I can face any of the frightening challenges life may throw my way. I will never close down my heart again. I can't, because my heart is where Caitlin will always live.

The lights flash and shimmer and the crowd roars as Andre begins a solid, slow thump on his bass. After a moment Ryan starts the sample of Caitlin's cello, a sound almost too good for this earth.

I breathe in the crisp, clean mountain air, and I reach out my fingers and begin to play along. I add my passion to Caitlin's, and all my friends join in with music of their own. We're together completely, riding the same wave, lost in the same magical spell.

This—this perfect moment, this music— is Caitlin's final gift to me. How happy she would have been to see all the dancers spread out before me, how thrilled she would have been to share in the joy her love has brought.

When my time comes, I sing:

Love never dies.
As long as the sun will rise,
love never dies.
Though you walk the edge of a knife,
live life. . . .

I sing it long and sweet, over the churning percussion, over Caitlin's repeating sample, investing the words with so much belief that I know it must settle into the heart of everyone who hears it. I sing it high and clipped, never forgetting that my message is joyful, that this song should make you love—and make you move.

The crowd is with me; I can feel them returning that love. And I let it fill me.

I will live my life, and part of Caitlin will always be mixed up in that life. Every time I feel something real—like now—she will be here with me.

Because true love never dies.

I immerse myself in the song that I wrote that day in my bedroom, the day when the impossibly wonderful sound of her cello returned me to living, returned me to love.

It's called "A Song for Caitlin."

Everyone enjoys a good love story, but the best ones come right out of real life! Did he win you over with charming words or steal your heart with his shy smile? When did you realize that he was the one? From the day you first met to the time you knew it was true love . . . you shared your stories with us, and now you can read all about the romantic moments of other readers.

"I needed a book on Kate Chopin for a paper I was writing about her, and the library had one copy. It wasn't on the shelf, and when I went to ask the librarian where it was, I saw this cute guy holding the book, waiting to borrow it. I begged him to let me take it out instead, and he said he would on one condition—that I would go out with him that weekend. I agreed, and I got the book and the guy."

—*Sylvia, 15*

"I was sketching this gorgeous guy in the park, and he noticed me looking at him. He walked by me and dropped a piece of paper in my lap. I looked at it—he'd written down his name and phone number. I called him, and we've been together ever since."

—*Michelle, 16*

"I applied for a job at this store, and I went in for an interview, but I ended up not getting the job. Then this guy who worked there called me late at night. He told me that he'd taken my number from my application because he'd seen me come in and thought I was pretty. I was so flattered, and even though I couldn't remember what he looked like at all, I agreed to go out with him. It turned out he was majorly hot! The date went great, and we just had our one-year anniversary."

—*Rochelle, 15*

"My lab partner in biology was really hot, and I'd had a crush on him for weeks. Then one day he asked me if I could help him study for a test we had on Monday. This guy knew much more than I did— I've never been a science person. So I figured maybe he was interested in me—and I was right! We went to a nice restaurant for our "study" date, and he never even brought up biology. We became a couple soon afterward, but unfortunately I didn't do that great on my exam!"

—*Stephanie, 15*

"I was totally obsessed with this guy, and I sometimes hung out with his good friend, Doug. Doug ended up asking me out. I was disappointed because I really wanted his friend, but then I went out with him anyway. To my surprise I fell head over heels in love with him. He won me over by all the sweet, thoughtful things he always did for me. We never would have been together if I'd had the guts to ask out his friend."

—*Rosie, 14*

"My boyfriend is supershy, so even though we'd been flirting with each other for a while, he was taking forever to ask me out. When he finally tried, he was so nervous that he mixed all his words up. Luckily I still figured out what he was asking, and I thought it was cool that I had that effect on him. We went out, and I was relieved to see that he soon loosened up enough to tell me how crazy about me he was."

—*Erica, 14*

"My boyfriend and I had been together for a few months when I turned sixteen. For my birthday we had tickets to a Fiona Apple concert, and it was really amazing because we got to hear 'our song' performed live. I was ready to tell him that I loved him that night, but then he started to cry because he wanted to tell me the same thing! He finally said it, and I told him that I felt the same way. Now whenever one of us hears that Fiona Apple song, we have to call the other to say 'I love you.'"

—*Reese, 16*

"On our anniversary my boyfriend brought me a book of love poems by Keats, my favorite poet. He also brought a big bag of jelly beans because he knew I was crazy about them. A lot of guys might stick to flowers and chocolate, but I liked how he actually took the time to find things that *I* loved."

—*Lynn, 14*

"On our first date, my boyfriend and I were walking through the park when it started to rain. Even though it was raining, the sun was still shining, so I said we should look for a rainbow. We never saw one, but at the end of the date my boyfriend said he loved seeing the rainbow. I didn't understand—we hadn't found it! He smiled and told me that *he* could see a rainbow from where he was, with me."

—*Lisa, 16*

"I was having problems with French, and my boyfriend was in the AP section. Every day he would give me a little note in French, with a romantic message. Then he would help me translate the words I didn't know yet. Suddenly I had a real motivation to learn because I wanted to be able to read his incredibly sweet letters without his help. It made it fun and exciting, and I started doing much better in my French class!"

—*JoAnn, 16*

Do you ever wonder about falling in love? About members of the opposite sex? Do you need a little friendly advice but have no one to turn to? Well, that's where we come in . . . Jenny and Jake. Send us those questions you're dying to ask, and we'll give you the straight scoop on life and love in the nineties.

DEAR JAKE

Q: *Keith was amazingly sweet to me when he was trying to get me to go out with him. He called me all the time, gave me little presents, and told me how beautiful I was. I finally agreed to date him, and we've been going out for a couple of weeks. Now he's not calling as often or doing all those great little things. Why is this?*

AR, Meredith, NY

A: This is a common problem; one of my female friends calls it the "cool-down syndrome." When a guy is going after you, he's in the warm-up stage—you know, working hard to impress you and prove that he's the one you want. Then you go out on a date or two, and it's the big test, the race itself. He runs the course, bringing you flowers and buying you a nice meal. Next you let him know that he won and you're his. This is when he starts slowing down, walking the last lap. Keith is convinced that he has your heart, so he no longer feels the need to push so hard. It's a good sign of his increased comfort with you as long as he is still keeping up an obvious interest level. I'm sure you'll start to cool down a little yourself—do you still obsess over every item of clothing (even the socks) that you wear when you see him?

Q: *I'm a senior, so I'm pretty busy with college applications. My boyfriend, Todd, is a junior, and he gets annoyed when I don't have enough time to spend with him. Why can't he understand that just because I don't have as much time right now doesn't mean that I don't still love him?*

JG, Minneapolis, MN

A: Although guys love to say that women are the ones who get jealous too easily and too often, we are in fact equally prone to attacks from the so-called green-eyed monster. Todd knows deep down that you love him, but he can't stand to face the possibility that anything else in your life could actually be more important to you than being with him.

There's also the factor that since he's younger than you, he doesn't understand how tough the application process is and how much time it takes up. Try to explain better exactly what you're working on so that he doesn't feel left out from this huge part of your life. Then schedule some nights for the two of you to be alone and talk about everything *but* college. As long as he's reassured that he's still "the center of your universe" (you can exaggerate a bit), everything should be fine.

DEAR JENNY

Q: *My best friend's ex-boyfriend, Craig, asked me out. I kind of want to say yes—is that totally wrong?*
SM, Montclair, NJ

A: Is it *totally* wrong? I don't know—that depends on some key factors. First off, how long was your friend dating Craig? How long ago did they break up? How serious were her feelings for him? Next you have to ask yourself, how serious are *your* feelings for this guy? If he meant a lot to your friend or the breakup was recent, it's probably a bad idea. The only reason worth considering this is if you truly believe you and Craig could have something very special. The best approach is to talk to your bud directly and see how she feels. Maybe she'll give you the green light, or maybe she'll tell you she'd rather you stayed away from her leftovers. Either way you won't feel like you're betraying someone you love if you're honest with her about your feelings.

Q: *I was head over heels in love with my first boyfriend, and he broke my heart when he ended things. Now I'm dating someone new, Andy. I like him a lot, but I don't feel the same way about him that I did about my first boyfriend. Does this mean Andy isn't right for me?*

AA, Bloomington, IL

A: Love is unique every time we experience it—there is a special way that we love our friends, our family, and the guys in our lives. However, we even feel a different type of love for people in the same categories; you will not love Andy in the same way that you loved your first boyfriend because he is a separate individual. This does not mean that what you feel for Andy is not still special or worthwhile.

It's possible that you're not in love with him or that he isn't the guy for you. But you need to judge this by looking at him as a person without comparing him to anyone from your past. Does Andy make you happy? Does your heart beat a little faster when you answer the phone and hear his voice? Trust yourself to know what is best for you, and don't worry about whether or not the feelings are the *same* as before—just make sure the feelings are good!

Do you have questions about love? Write to:
Jenny Burgess or Jake Korman
c/o Daniel Weiss Associates
33 West 17th Street
New York, NY 10011

Don't miss any of the books in *Love Stories*
—the romantic series from Bantam Books!